If There is
DYNAMITE
in You Here is
THE FUSE

A. L. Kitselman

Originally published as
If There is DYNAMITE in You Here is THE FUSE by P.B.A.
by The Translator's Press
Thirty East Sixtieth Street
New York City
Copyright 1946 by
THE TRANSLATOR'S PRESS
U. S. and International Copyright Secured

New edition published in the USA and the UK
by

MASTERWORKS INTERNATIONAL
27 Old Gloucester Street
London
WC1N 3XX
UK

Email: admin@mwipublishing.com
Web: http:/www.mwipublishing.com

ISBN: 978-0-9927706-9-3
copyright © A. L. Kitselman 1946, 2015

Cover by mwidesign.com
© Morag Campbell/Dreamstime/Peter Sjokvist/Sahua

Contents

Alva la Salle 'Beau' Kitselman age 22,
at Stanford University Summer 1936

WARNING

There are two kinds of evil—doing things which should not be done, and not doing things which should be done. Many who avoid the former are guilty of the latter. This is the story of a man who avoided both. It is a true story; parts of it happened before these words were written down, other parts have happened since, and still others parts are happening now. The persons involved in the story are living at the time of this writing, and their accomplishments are as described.

Some are offended by the nakedness described in these pages; they are those who are not particularly proud of the things they have done while naked. Let them be reassured; nakedness is not offensive to the morally sound.

Some are shocked at the openness and sincerity with which intimate subjects are discussed. This cannot be helped; they are subjects which should be discussed, and it would be evil to avoid doing what should be done. If sincerity and openness necessitate an apology, it will not be found here.

A great many are alarmed at the idea of a man involved with three women at once. That is understandable, for so was the man himself. He is thankful to this day that there were no more than three! This story is told as it happened, not as might be thought best. Names have been altered, of course, but little else.

A final warning to the reader:

There is no evil in this book; yet, as you read it, it may seem evil, because there are things in it which may be associated with evil in your mind. Be patient and persevere, and you will find that it is an account of actions so far from evil as to be almost incredible, and a message to you as an individual concerning your future.

I.

Jedediah Strong paced back and forth in his hotel room. It was nearly dawn. He had undressed hours before, taken a very hot shower bath, and was cooling off before going to bed. He was taller than average, well-proportioned, and about thirty years old. He had left his hair roughed up after drying it, so that it was wild, like the mane of a lion. His skin was still radiating heat, and appeared to glow when he passed in front of the dark windows. His body walked as if it were a healthy animal being exercised on a leash—a naked man-animal.

After a while Strong suddenly realized that his body had cooled down to room temperature, and this recalled him to his surroundings. He sat down on the bed, lost himself in thought again for a few minutes, and finally slid in under the covers. He did not turn out the light, however, but folded his hands behind his head and stared in the direction of the ceiling for quite some time. Finally a point was reached at which the thinking could he put aside, for a hand was stretched out to pick up the telephone and inquire the time, but—there was no telephone. He remembered why; the hotel was crowded and he had been given a furnished alcove to use as a room. He turned away from the table which had no phone on it and saw on the other side of his bed the curtains which separated his alcove from the main hotel corridor. Then he thought he remembered seeing a clock at the end of the corridor, and decided that all he had to do to learn the time was to lean out of the curtains and look down the hall. The curtains opened near the foot of the bed, so Strong sat up, leaned forward, pulled the curtain back and looked out.

The first thing he saw was that the 'clock' down the corridor was not a clock but the elevator floor-indicator. The second thing he saw was that the curtains were moving! Not the curtains, but something under the curtains next to his bed. He said, "Hey" and the motion became more rapid. Three crawling shapes materialized at the end of the curtain, rose up suddenly and became the backs of three bathrobe-clad female forms rapidly hurrying down the hall.

Strong called out, "Come back here!" even as he realized he had been spied upon.

The three backs seemed to writhe with fear and excitement as his voice reached them, but they continued to hurry down the hall. By this time, however, Strong had his wits about him. He raised his voice slightly and called,

"Come back here, or I'll tell!"

The hurry seemed to slowly drain out of the disappearing bathrobe clad forms. They slowed down and stopped, but they did not turn around. His voice lower now, Strong said,

"Come on, come back here, or I'll tell the whole place what you've been doing!"

The figures turned, faces looking almost straight at the floor. They came down the hall as if pulled by cables, unresisting but yet unwilling—three teenage girls, almost dying of embarrassment. As they came down the hall, Strong reached back and pulled on his bathrobe. By the time the three shrinking figures reached the curtain opening, Strong was standing there waiting for them. He pulled each into the alcove, and then closed the curtains.

"Now," he said, "whatever happens in here is a secret, you understand, unless you choose otherwise. If you make any outcry, and people find you here, you will lose something which may be more precious to you than anything else—your reputations. Think that over a little bit."

He pushed two of his guests onto the edge of his bed and shoved the third into a chair.

"There isn't anything that I am likely to do to you that isn't natural and more or less to be expected, sooner or later, but if you decide you don't like it and call out, you'll find that what society will do to you isn't even human. I think you know that as well as I do, so don't forget it." The three girls said nothing, hut the attitude of their hunched shoulders and bowed heads indicated that they felt completely helpless in the hands of a man who, in their opinion, had every right to punish their transgression as he saw fit. Furthermore, they were well-formed young women, and they had been caught by a strange man in an intrusion which in their eyes denied them all rights except the rights of captive women. And what are the rights of captive women? Simply the command of beautiful flesh that it be noticed and, willing or not, be made to answer its natural purpose.

After a moment Strong spoke again, more gently.

"There is one thing—it is not necessary for you to blush, for there is nothing shameful in what you have done—except in the eyes of the world outside that curtain. You were curious about the body of man and with good reason, because there are forces within you that lead you in that direction. What is shameful is that healthy young women should have to go spying to learn about man—and that is the world's shame, not yours! I am glad you came. I will do what I please with you, and you will accomplish your purpose; you will learn about man. So look straight into my eyes and have no thought of fear; I think you can tell by the sound of my voice that I am not cruel."

One by one the girls lifted their heads and looked at him. Strong looked intently into the face of each in turn. The air was electric, but shame was gone.

"Do you wonder at the force which brought you here?" Strong asked, almost as if talking to himself. "Why look here, right in front of us, how powerful it is!"

He turned to the dark-haired young woman he had pushed into the chair.

"The force is indeed in you, little beauty with the hair of night! All your life you have been learning how to attract men—and now, when according to most standards you should be endeavouring to look as unattractive as possible, see how you sit in that chair as enticingly as if you posed for it! I can and will do exactly what I please with you, all right. You are ready for it!"

The three girls looked at each other in silent amazement. It was true. Without a conscious thought about it, the brunette girl had arranged herself so as to appear her best when seen from Strong's direction.

Strong studied each of them silently. He seemed indifferent to the passage of time. The darkness outside the windows was beginning to lessen. The young women were now studying Strong in return, as if the passing minutes were helping them to realize and accept the relationship which had come upon them. Because they had lost all power to resist him, they were no longer afraid of him, and were beginning to experience that internal ecstasy which women attain when they become perfectly receptive and subject to the will of man. The most tranquil of the three was apparently the oldest, perhaps nineteen or twenty, and in many ways a young woman of uncommon beauty. Strong had already called her 'the silver one' in his mind, for not only her silver-gold hair but her eyes and the texture of her skin gave the impression of silver. Moreover, she had that rare beauty of line in her body which is so much more than just a good figure. No matter how she stood or sat, she was a picture of stillness and beauty.

The other two girls were attractive in a more obvious way. One was a lovely auburn-haired girl with a rose-petal complexion, and the other was a little olive-skinned brunette not over eighteen, apparently the youngest of the three. Both were attractive in a provocative way, but the auburn-haired girl, although a temptation in body and manner, had some of the dignity of the silver girl, whereas the little olive skinned one was not only a temptation but a challenge. Of course, almost all healthy girls are beautiful in their late teens, but the silver girl was still something special. Her eyes told Strong that she had accepted him, not because of the situation, but because she was of high quality and recognized him to be such. Finally, Strong walked toward the oldest girl, who rose as he came near her.

"I will take you first," he said.

"Please, mister, not Joan!" the auburn-haired girl pleaded as she rushed to the side of her friend. "She didn't want to come; we talked her into it!"

Then the little dark girl spoke.

"To be perfectly honest, mister, neither of these girls had anything to do with it. This whole thing was my idea, and I am the one who got them to come."

"I am glad you did," said Strong. "I like them. Well, Joan?"

The girl called Joan turned to her companions.

"I am not afraid of this man. He will do what he pleases with me, but what am I for if not that? Some man will get me sooner or later, and how do I know that this one is not as good as any? He has spoken to us honestly enough; what did we come for if not to learn about man? I think that this man is probably better than any we are likely to get and I do not think he will hurt us. Yes," and she turned back to Strong, "I am ready for you, sir."

There was a couch on the other side of the alcove, next to the window. Strong took each of the other two girls by the arm and walked them over to it; then he returned to Joan. He stood facing her for a moment, and the air around them seemed to become unbearably bright. Then he said softly,

"I am taking you first, Joan, because you have courage."

Joan did not know exactly how Strong approached her. Gradually she became aware that she was being supported in his arms, that the secrets of her mouth were being taken from her, and that her entire body had become a sea of incandescence. She never knew that her arms were encircling Strong as tenderly as his arms were about her; she felt only that his body and hers had become a molten mass. Then in some way time got started again and there was an impression of being carried to the bed and then she felt the touch of cool sheets all over her body. Sheets? Hadn't she had a bathrobe on? Bathrobe? The thought was too cumbersome and she let it fade as her nerves or something began to uncurl in the coolness of the bed. Then in a moment the bed moved a little and she felt a warmth beside her and she knew the man was near again. A strange kind of lightning shot through her body in liquid flashes, a fire started in her mouth and in several other places where the man was touching her, her bones turned to water and she became a small strangling universe entirely surrounded by man. Then she and the man ran together in a kind of warm calmness and began to cool and there was a little air and the bed was there and it was quiet, and slowly her body appeared and the man was carrying her and putting her on a couch and covering her with the bathrobe, and his voice said in her ear, "You have not been harmed, Joan, and neither will they be. Just lie here and feel," and kisses touched her eyes and forehead and that was all.

Strong handled each of the girls in a different way, and yet their internal experiences were substantially the same. Before long Joan felt herself lifted up, helped into her bathrobe and put into the cushioned chair. Though her eyes were open, she was only beginning to use them. She saw Strong carry Claire from the bed to the couch, bend over her a moment as he covered her up, and then stride across the room to olive-skinned Ada, but the actions were not very real to her. She saw Ada stand challengingly before Strong like the little minx she was, saw him respond by stripping her as naked as seemed natural for her, and still the provocative little creature posed as impudently as before. She realized that Ada was the same with or without clothes. She saw Strong send Ada into the bed without embracing her, and she marvelled at the independent and seductive way in which the little witch obeyed.

12

Ada was excited and unresisting, but she was a provocation even then. Joan could not see what went on in the bed, and she had no clear idea herself; nevertheless, there was no doubt in her mind that Ada was not being neglected.

Though she hadn't thought about it yet, she was aware that she couldn't be objective about Strong. To her, he was 'the man" or, more simply, MAN, a kind of universal force. After a while the bed became still, and she saw Strong beckoning to her. Rather dreamily she drifted over to him, dropped her robe to the floor, and crawled in beside him. It felt so good to be close to him, with her head on his shoulder. Ada's head was on his other shoulder. The two heads, before long, were fast asleep.

II.

Jedediah Strong lay in bed looking at the ceiling. To his right a girl with hair like darkness lay sleeping on his shoulder; to his left a girl like an ingot of silver slept close against his side. Across the room a girl with a rose-petal skin was dreaming on a couch. Outside, the birds had begun to sing about the coming light of day. Strong did not look sleepy; on the contrary, he seemed lost in leisurely thought, just as before. It could be seen in his eyes that he was a man who enjoyed the process of thinking and liked to give his time to it.

After a while his face lost its appearance of abstract thought and took on a more purposeful expression. He turned his head to the sleeping brunette on his right and woke her with a rather thoroughgoing kiss. The girl responded like a healthy animal and snuggled close against his side. Then he turned to the silver-skinned beauty on his left and woke her in the same way, except perhaps more tenderly. Then he said to her,

"Joan, will you call the girl on the couch?"

Quietly she called, "Claire. Claire. Wake up, Claire. Wake up!"

The auburn-haired girl opened her eyes, stretched, and sat up. The blanket with which Strong had covered her fell back as she did so, and her rose-petal nakedness was beautiful to see.

"Claire," said Strong. "will you put on your robe and come sit close by the bed? I want to tell you something."

It was plain that Claire was still in a very dreamy condition, but she managed to get into her bathrobe and move the large chair next to the bed.

"I want to tell you a story about what we have been doing," Strong said. "Are you awake enough to hear it now?"

All three heads nodded, so Strong continued.

"When you three were watching me walk back and forth a while ago, I was indulging in a habit of mine. I don't know how long ago I acquired it, but it makes my life interesting. It is the habit of thinking about the question: 'What is the most intelligent thing to do?' I spend hours at it. When I accidentally discovered that I had company, I was surprised and said, "Hey!" Then, between that time and when I started calling you back, I thought to myself, these three girls are virgin, or they would not have been so curious about a man. Their curiosity might get them into serious trouble. So I stopped you and called you back, because it is my disposition to intrude into other people's lives when I see them heading for trouble. After you were in here and I saw that you all had beauty of face and body, were nearly twenty years old, and felt so ashamed of what you had done, I realized that you must have lived extremely sheltered lives, for otherwise you would have been so pawed and mauled around by amorous young males that you would not be capable of feeling such shame or such curiosity about man. Then I got started on my habit again and thought, what is the most intelligent thing to do? If I just let these girls go, with or without a lecture, the force within them is so strong that it will get them into a similar situation with some other man, and this other man may be capable of hurting them morally or physically, which I am not. So I cannot let them go.

Then I thought, 'Why are they here?' Is it not because they have serious need of knowledge about man? How can I give them such knowledge in such a way that they suffer no harm thereby?

And then I thought of something which seemed the most intelligent thing to do, and I did it. It was not an easy thing for me to do, but there is a reason which I have not told you, and I am satisfied with what I have done.

This is what I have done: When you entered this room you were virgins. You have each had a complete experience of the relationship between man and woman. You were utterly helpless at the time, and probably have no clear idea of exactly what was done to you, but by now you should be awake enough to know that you are still virgins! You are physically intact, yet you have experienced the emotional equivalent of rape.

Now it is my intention to teach you as much as you can learn about yourselves and about man, so that you can live your lives intelligently. First, however, I want to know how you feel about what I have already done. Does it seem to you that I have wronged you in any way? If it does, all I can do is apologize most sincerely, for I have acted with only the kindest of motives. Joan, what do you think?"

The silver girl raised her head and looked down into Strong's face without saying a word. Then, slowly, and with infinite tenderness, she gave her heart to him—in a kiss. When finally she raised her head again, the eyes into which she looked were a trifle misty, and in a voice that was not quite steady Strong said,

"You have told me, Joan. I want them to know what you think, too. Will you tell them?"

Joan smiled at him, then turned and spoke to Claire and Ada.

"This man took me into a world of fire so intense that I had no self-control whatever, and was not even conscious of my actions. I know he felt it, too, because he was there with me. All I can say is that if he can keep his head and be considerate of others under circumstances which reduce me to complete incoherence,—well, I love him."

Joan's face was radiant as she said this, and she gave Strong another kiss. This time he did not speak after being so honored, but his eyes were eloquent. Finally, after Joan had settled happily hack on his shoulder, he said,

"Claire, what do you have to say?"

The auburn-haired girl stood up and leaned over the bed to answer Strong.

"Mister" she said, "if you were single and unattached, I would like to be your wife. I think you are something very special. But I want to belong to one man only, and I want that man to be all mine. I appreciate what you have done for me, because without your help I might have gotten into serious trouble, and I thank you especially for leaving my body intact, for I want to be a virgin bride. But will you really teach me about myself and about men? I would like to know how to find the best possible husband, and how to be as good a bride as he deserves."

"Yes, Claire," Strong answered, "I will teach you what you want to know."

"Then there is one thing I wish to say. I don't want you to lie there between those two brazen creatures and think I'm not affectionate. If it weren't for the fact that I'm determined to save myself for my husband I'd be in that bed somewhere, too, and just as close to you as Joan and Ada. To be perfectly honest, I feel rather neglected."

"I understand, Claire."

Strong's voice was gentle. "Look, do you think your husband would object to your having a sweetheart?"

The auburn-haired girl had been close to tears, but now her face cleared and she said,

"Why, no, I don't see why he should. A girl has to have some attention."

"Then listen. You are very beautiful, Claire, and I love you. If I were single and unattached, I would like to be your husband, but that cannot be. Still, I love you. Do you think we might be sweethearts? You don't have to answer now, dear; it is rather sudden. Think it over for three or four seconds, beloved, and then give me the answer I want so much to hear."

"You dog! You know exactly what I want! Yes, we can be sweethearts, but how can there be any romance to it when you lie there in a bed full of naked women and grin at me like a Cheshire cat? What a sweetheart!" and the tears almost came again.

Suddenly Strong sat up, pulled Claire close to him, and kissed away the tears that sparkled in her eyes. "I won't tease you any more, Claire," he soothed, "and I know how to see to it that no naked women can come between us."

He lifted her up on the bed so that she lay right on top of him.

"There," he said, "all that separates us now is a bathrobe, a sheet, and a blanket. We've had our first quarrel, dear, and we mustn't let it grow cold."

Before long the beauteous Claire had kissed and been kissed until she no longer had any reason to feel neglected. The bed was a little crowded now, what with Joan on the left, Ada on the right, Strong in the middle, and Claire on top. Strong was a male man, so he didn't mind being completely surrounded by beauty. Joan and Ada didn't seem to care, and Claire had been kissed into contentedness.

"Well, Ada," said Strong, "it's your turn."

The little dark haired girl raised her head and looked at the other three.

"I don't think, Joan would mind, but I understand how Claire feels, so I won't indulge in any demonstrations just now. Mister, you're all right. I think you know what you're doing, and as far as I'm concerned, you can do anything you like with me. The next time you feel like doing anything, just let me know. Those may not be the most moral sentiments in the world, but they're mine."

"You're all right yourself, Ada," said Strong. "You may not be the most spiritual girl I have met, but you're certainly not the least honest."

"And now, ladies" he went on, "there will be traffic in the corridor before long. Much as I dislike the idea, we'll have to separate for a while. I judge from your lack of concern about the time that you are here at the hotel unchaperoned—is that right?"

They all answered at once, but the gist of it was that their people were all in Washington on government business and had sent them to the Park for a vacation on their own, provided that all three stay close together.

"All right then," said Strong, "let's all get some sleep. I will be gone from the hotel until late this evening. Will you be in your rooms at about ten o'clock tonight?"

They would, it seemed.

"May I drop by at that time for a visit?" Strong wanted to know. He might.

It was settled. They all got up—first Joan, then Claire, Strong, and Ada last of all. Strong took Joan to the curtain opening first. They did not embrace, perhaps out of consideration for Claire, but stood for a moment looking at each other in such a way as to imply that no embrace was necessary. Then Strong looked out to see if the way was clear, and in a moment Joan had gone. His parting with Claire was different. Joan loved him; for her no demonstrations were necessary. But Claire was in love with him; she wanted romance. Strong held her in his arms and kissed her face and neck; all of which made her seem to glow with beauty. Soon she, too, had gone.

When Strong turned to say good-bye to Ada, he was somewhat startled to find that she had thrown her robe over the end of the bed and was standing there as seductively as she knew how. She waited just long enough for him to feel the impact of the picture she made, then she ran forward, slipped into the front of his bathrobe, put her arms around his neck and gave him her demonstration. It nearly knocked him of his feet; the little witch was charged with a high potential of animal sexuality. The touch of her lips and body caused him to experience a burning sensation that was almost painful.

Ada made her 'demonstration' last just long enough to put a good-sized dent in Strong's self-control, then she slipped out of his arms, into her robe, and was gone. Strong stood there dizzily for a moment, while mentally giving out a long, low whistle, then he took of his bathrobe and crawled into bed. He was tired. As he went to sleep, his last thoughts were of how much like a mirror he had become. In his mind it looked like this:

Joan loves me	and I love her
Claire is in love with me	and I am in love with her
Ada wants me	and I want her

And so he went to sleep.

III.

Precisely at ten o'clock Jedediah Strong knocked at the door of a hotel room; three nervous voices yelled simultaneously,

"Come in!"

He quickly opened the door, slipped inside, shut it behind him, and started to raise his finger to his mouth and say "Sh!" That was as far as he got. Three excited bodies hit him at the same instant, six frantic arms were thrown around his neck, and three strained faces sought to reach his. If it had not been for his height, four heads would have banged together. For a moment he could not speak because the breath had been knocked out of him; three girls can weigh more than three hundred pounds. Fortunately for Strong, the girls themselves saw what they had done and backed away shamefacedly.

"Please forgive us," cried Ada.

"We couldn't help it," added Joan.

"We were so worried," said Claire.

Then they all talked at once until Strong signalled for them to stop.

"You'll just have to let me talk to you one at a time," he pleaded, "and have got to get my breath before I can do even that. You almost got me just then—for a second or two I thought my time had come!"

He sat down in a chair and the three young women stood in a semicircle before him—Joan on the left, Claire in the middle, and Ada on the right. Each was wearing a negligee but Strong did not see what they wore. He saw only the clear simplicity of love in Joan's beautiful eyes, the glow of romantic happiness in Claire's rose-petal face, and the eager, hungry awareness of him that seemed to radiate from Ada's body. Each was beautiful in her own way.

"Joan, will you tell me the reason for all the violence?"

"It's very simple," she answered. "We were afraid you might not come. We love you and we are dependent upon you. The day has been empty without you, and the fear that we might not see you again has not been pleasant. We have been sitting here watching this door for at least an hour, and we counted the minutes until ten o'clock."

Strong's voice was tender as he said,

"I have been counting the minutes, too."

Then he turned to Claire, who said,

"Joan might have added that she had more faith in you than we did. Ada and I both had our doubts, but Joan said she would rather believe in you and be wrong than doubt you and be right. She made me ashamed of my selfishness and jealousy, and I've decided not to be that way about you anymore. Joan and Ada think as much of you as I do, and from now on you can kiss them right in front of me whenever you wish. I may not like it, but I won't object."

"I think there is a way around that little difficulty, Claire. It's a good resolution, anyway."

Strong's appreciation of Claire was apparent in his eyes, and her response to his eyes made her lovely. Then he turned to Ada.

"There is one thing they didn't mention," said Ada, "and that is that we had a little romance in mind when we came on this trip. When we arrived yesterday some of the boys here looked pretty good to us, but today we couldn't even see them because we were so busy daydreaming about you. I don't know what you've done to us, mister, but you're it! You'd better not let us down or we're sure to do something wicked on the rebound. You've just got to stay with us!"

"I won't desert you, Ada!" said Strong. "I won't desert any of you. I went away today because I had to let you find out how you feel about me. I have been thinking about you all day. May I see each of you alone for a few minutes?"

It was agreed upon; Claire and Ada went into the next room and Joan remained with Strong. He stood facing her for a moment, and the air grew bright again. Then, as before, she found herself in his arms, and the room fell away into space. Joan was not unconscious; a part of her mind was quite aware when Strong carried her to the easy chair, sat down, and held her in his arms. It was just that her ability to experience happiness was such that she lost all interest in external consciousness at such times. She heard Strong's voice in her ear.

"Joan, this that you feel is fire. You are full of it, and it will take you to the peak of happiness. I know the way to that happiness and I will help you find it."

He held her close to him, as tenderly as if she were an angel from heaven, until her consciousness returned to normal. The relationship between these two was so deep that it made no sign on the surface; for them, romance and sensuality were simply not adequate means of expression. After a while Strong uttered one word, "Claire," and Joan got up and left the room.

Claire came in as if she were meeting a sweetheart in a garden, all radiant with expectancy. Strong stretched out his hands to clasp hers, stood looking at her for a moment, then swept her suddenly into a most dramatic embrace.

"You are very beautiful, Claire," he said, and kissed her. "I am so happy that we are sweethearts!"

He seemed to know that Claire needed affection and adoration just as some people need food, and he gave her just what she wanted. Each kiss seemed to make her more lovely, until finally her radiance became tranquil and satisfied. Beauty had been fed. He held her on his lap as if he were visiting his best girl in her parlor, and they talked.

"Do you realize that I don't even know your name?" she half-pouted.

"In that case, my dear," he smiled, "permit me to introduce myself. My name is Jedediah Strong, and I am the proud lover of a most beautiful lady. And who might you be, miss?"

"I am Claire King," she told him, "and I am the sweetheart of a most masterful man, who expects me to be unselfish and share him with other women."

She started to get up, but Strong pulled her back on his lap.

"Not so fast, my pretty maid. You forget how masterful I am," and the rose-petal skin was kissed into radiance again. Claire left as if she had just been with a sweetheart in a garden.

When Ada came in, Strong came up to her and held her by the arms, so that she could not touch him with her body.

"Now listen, you little volcano." he said in a voice deliberately kept low, "I don't want any more salesmanship. I'm sold. You want me and I want you, so take it easy. There are certain parts of this 'wanting' business that are dangerous and we're going to do this right, or not at all, do you understand? Besides, it will be much better if we take our time."

With a curious smile, Ada shrugged aside his arms and stepped back a pace.

"All right. Man. You do the timing."

She said the word "man" as if it were a complete sentence.

"I don't care how slow or fast we go, just so we arrive. I want you, and it can be either here and now, or later and somewhere else. As long as I know that you want me, I can wait."

"Then there is something I want right now, Ada." Strong's voice was still low and deliberate. "I want an appetizer, just an appetizer, and not the entire dinner."

A sudden mystery veiled Ada's eyes.

"Try me," she said softly, and Strong discovered that she possessed an amazing intelligence in her body. She was wearing a negligee of black lace, and she stood there like a statue of woman's responsiveness. He walked around her and looked her over, and though she did not move, he could feel her consciousness meet his wherever he looked. He touched her here and there as he looked, as if his fingers wished to verify what his eyes beheld, and she spoke to him silently through the curves of her flesh, saying, this living body has experience only when and where you experience it. These contours and this flesh know no other reality than to be seen and used by you. Without you, man, this flesh is mindless clay; it depends upon you for its life. Finally, he kissed her, and while he did so his hands conducted her body in a symphony of sexual awareness. Ada had not known before that there could be subtlety in sex; to her it had seemed only a strong force to be expressed in violence. Now she learned that her body was like a well-tuned orchestra capable of responding in delicate harmonies to the subtle touch of a skilled hand. There was nothing violent or even very anatomical about what Strong was doing to her—just a touch here and a gentle pressure there, and all with the attitude of a man painting a masterpiece, concentrated, detached. She realized that he was teaching her with his hands, teaching her the meaning of subtlety, harmony, and depth of feeling. It was so beautiful that suddenly there were tears in her eyes, and then he held her gently in his arms until she was as still and tranquil as a midnight pool.

"You are a beautiful woman, Ada," he said. "Your body is an unknown world, a place of mystery and enchantment. No man should come near it who does not know this" She knew in her heart that his words and the truth he had shown her had saved her forever from the danger of becoming cheap.

Joan and Claire were called in, and the three girls sat on the edge of the bed. Strong pushed his chair up near the bed and sat facing them.

"I said that I would teach you about yourselves and about man," he said. "Let us begin now. Last night you learned something about the power and beauty of the relationship which can exist between man and woman. Yet you were forced into that relationship. Insofar as you were subject to my will and unable to help yourselves, you were raped. Now how can rape be beautiful? In the answer to this question can be found one of the most important differences between man and woman.

You have probably read many stories in which a hero and a villain fight over who shall have the beautiful heroine. The hero usually triumphs over the villain, the heroine falls into his arms, and with or without benefit of clergy they go to bed together and live happily forever after. Many of these stories are historically true; others are fiction. Most of us have read so many of them that we think they represent the true nature of things; we assume that the heroine is always rescued in the 'nick of time'. This belief in the 'nick of time' theory is responsible for much of the moral confusion existing in the world today. The average person has no idea what the heroine should do if the hero misses his cue.

Nature, however, solved the problem long ago. The only historical romances that are published for the average reader are those that are successful according to the 'nick of time' criterion; the hero always arrives before it is 'too late'. However, there are as many, if not more, true historical romances which do not measure up to the 'nick of time' standard; the hero didn't make it, perhaps because he got lost or delayed, perhaps because villains are frequently more skilled at violence than peace-loving heroes. In these true cases, what happened to the heroines?

Some preferred death to rape, and of these there were three classes: those who wanted to destroy themselves but could not bring themselves to do it (the largest class), those who wanted to but could find no way of doing so, and those who wanted to destroy themselves and succeeded (the smallest class). All the rest preferred rape to death.

You may say that this is not a pleasant thing to talk about; it isn't. Nevertheless, thousands upon thousands of your female ancestors have been raped; there is probably no one living today who is not descended from rape. Gentleness and violence have always been with us, and rape is merely the violent aspect of sex.

At some future time we shall talk about the problem of rape as a possibility in every woman's life; just at present I want to emphasize one way in which rape has contributed to the emotional character of woman. It is this: nature has adapted the sexual mechanism of woman to her environment. Every normal woman can respond either voluntarily or involuntarily; she can satisfy either the hero or the villain and enjoy the process. Naturally there is a difference in a woman's ability to respond to a man of acceptable or unacceptable person, but, other things being equal, a hero is a lover who asks permission and a villain is one who does not.

This amoral nature is the standard equipment with which women start their life. Moral training can change it for the better; immoral training can make it worse. This is an important difference between man and woman, because man's nature is almost entirely voluntary; men are not raped. They may be seduced, but I know of only one case in all history in which a woman raped a man.

Now what does this difference mean? It means that woman is more responsive to her environment than man is, and that man is more resistant to external influence than woman is. Woman is normally moral or immoral according to her environment; man is normally whatever he is regardless of his environment. A woman may be moral or immoral by turns indiscriminately; a man is more likely to be either one or the other and slow to change. Environment can quickly improve or corrupt a woman, whereas a man is not easily altered. A bad man is worse than an equally bad woman because it is harder to improve him. On the other hand, a good man is better than an equally good woman, because he is less corruptible.

Women in general seem to be aware of their amoral nature, usually subconsciously, and most of them adopt one of three ways of living with it. Some women seem to say,

'Well, it is my nature to be amoral, so that's the way I'll live.' Others apparently have decided,

'I will suppress the immoral side of my nature and try to be a moral woman.'

Still others impress me as having this attitude:

'The nature of woman at best is weak and corruptible; I want to be free of all its limitations.' "

At this point Strong paused for a moment or two, and then he said,

"You don't need to tell me which ways you have chosen. I knew last night."

The three girls smiled at him reflectively. They knew he knew.

IV.

Jedediah Strong stood up and looked down at the three girls sitting before him.

"Joan," he said, "how long can your vacation last?"

"We have all summer," Joan replied.

"Claire, do you think that if your parents knew me, they would entrust you in my keeping?"

Claire thought a moment before she answered.

"If they knew us well, and knew you well. I think they would feel that we are safer with you than without you."

"Ada, had the three of you made specific plans about how to spend your vacation?"

Ada glanced at the other girls and then said,

"If we did, we can't remember them. We haven't the slightest idea what to do, unless you tell us."

Strong smiled.

"I will make your plans for you. I am going to take you away with me into another world, a world not related to the twentieth century as you know it. You will be able to communicate with your parents so that they will not worry about you, but in all other respects you are going to vanish from the face of the earth."

"But where are you taking us?"

The words seemed to burst from an anxious and bewildered Claire.

"We are going to visit the Place of the Ancient Fish," Strong answered.

"But where is that?" asked Ada, who was now bewildered also

"It is in the Country of the Water People" was Strong's enigmatic reply.

"How do we get there?" Joan inquired, her attitude indicating nothing more than interest and curiosity. Joan would have cheerfully entered the gates of hell at the side of the man she loved.

"We travel through the bed of a forgotten sea."

By this time Claire thought she knew how to get a reasonable answer out of the mysterious Strong. Triumphantly she asked what she thought was a shrewd question.

"Where do we go first?"

"We go first to the Mountains of the Moon," said Strong, and Claire and the other girls all had to laugh at her unsuccessful attempt to clarify the situation. Strong smiled at Claire and then continued,

"There is a good reason for all this mystery, so please be patient with it. We will leave here tomorrow morning. You may each take one suitcase only; our ship was not built for four. Leave your other baggage here at the hotel. You will need no civilized clothes; bring only what you would wear on a hike in desert mountain country. I will help you write to your parents and make any other necessary arrangements."

Naturally the girls were excited and wanted to talk all at once about the trip, but Strong stopped them before they got started.

"You will have time to talk and pack tomorrow morning," he said, "tonight there are other things to do. First, there is something I must explain to you about yourselves while we are still in this environment, and then I am going to see to it that you get a good night's sleep. So forget the trip until tomorrow morning; you will have time enough then to think about it."

The three young women had become quiet while Strong was speaking; their interest in him made them almost instantly responsive to his wishes. He went back to his chair and sat down. Leisurely he studied each of the three eager faces, and, when satisfied that things were just right, he spoke again.

"I have explained to you one of the reasons why women excel men in their response to moral training, and also why they need more of it. Another reason is that a man who wants to achieve true morality will go a long way toward training himself, whereas self-training is more difficult for women. These are reasons based upon the emotional difference between men and women; there are also reasons of a social and physical nature. I will tell you some of them tonight."

"Ada, come here!"

Strong used a tone of command because he knew that Ada wanted that tone from him. The beautiful dark-haired girl came and stood before him, as submissive as a slave woman. Indeed, her alluring and articulate body in its sheath of black lace made her seem like a lovely concubine awaiting her master's pleasure, and in her heart she was just that.

Nevertheless, in spite of his effort to be imperious, Strong's voice was somewhat tender as he spoke to her.

"That is a beautiful negligee you are wearing, Ada. Take it off."

The words were spoken without emphasis but in a tone of casual command such as a great lord might use in addressing his favorite dancing girl. Something electric went through Ada's body and a look of happiness appeared in her eyes as if she had been waiting for just such a moment. Without display and without modesty she slipped out of her negligee, and remained clothed in her eloquent nakedness.

"Now come sit on my lap," said Strong. "I am going to use you as a guinea pig, Ada."

He held her on his lap as if she were a lecture exhibit, and then he began his lecture.

"This," he said, pointing to Ada's body, "is public commodity number one. It is important to understand its place in nature and its significance in the modern world. Woman's body is a toy, the most popular of all toys. It has a life of its own, apart from woman's mind. It likes to be played with."

As he spoke, Strong treated Ada's body as he might treat a toy. He bent and unbent her legs and arms, turned her head up and down and from side to side, doubled her up into a bundle and straightened her out again. His performance was deliberately intended to resemble that of a child with a new plaything and the demonstration was a complete success, because it was obvious that Ada enjoyed the process of being handled. Having made his point, he continued.

"Nature has fashioned this body in the form of an attractive toy because it serves as bait in the process of reproducing the species. It is a toy to man because his body likes to play with it and his mind likes to own it; it is a toy to woman because her body likes to be a toy and because her mind likes to play with it just as if it were a doll. Did you ever notice that when girls stop playing with dolls, they begin doing to their bodies all the things that they formerly did to the dolls? They dress and ornament their bodies endlessly, parade and pose them before mirrors and other people, and indeed spend most of their lives doing for their bodies exactly what they would do for a beautiful doll.

"Some men know how to handle the toys which are women's bodies; the majority do not. Women whose bodies have never been handled properly develop an attitude of mind that is appropriate to their condition. To them the toy is not a source of pleasure, so they learn to take pleasure in the power it gives them over men. These women have exactly the same attitude toward their bodies that an organ grinder has toward his monkey. The organ grinder does not love the monkey, or else would not treat it as he does; to him the monkey is a means of livelihood and nothing more, He knows that people are fascinated by the monkey, and though he has contempt for them, he lets them fondle the monkey and play with it, if they make it worth his while. This is not a very nice way to live, but all attractive women who are sexually unsatisfied live in this way. All such women prostitute their bodies—some for money, some for attention, some for security, some for a home and a family and some just to pass the time.

There is a simple test whereby a woman may determine whether or not she prostitutes herself. If she at any time thinks or speaks of 'letting' a male touch her, kiss her, or make love to her, then she is one of those unfortunate women whose bodies do not receive proper handling. The great majority of sexually eligible women fall in this category.

Many women devote so much attention to the toys which are their bodies that they go through life almost completely oblivious of the fact that they also have minds. The embrace of a woman's mind is far more important to a man than the pleasures of her body, for the mind of a responsive and sensitive woman can calm and cool a man, whereas the body of a dull-minded woman can never give satisfaction. The subtlety of the mental and emotional relationship between man and woman is a most mysterious thing to contemplate.

You are three women sitting here before me. Physically, you are entities capable of receiving my physical being in an embrace so nearly complete that it may profoundly influence our lives. Yet mentally and emotionally, at this very moment, you are receiving my mental being, my words and thought, into your minds in an embrace no less complete. This relation between us is so profound that it is influencing our lives perhaps far more deeply than could any physical embrace, and yet the majority of people cannot see that sexual completeness and responsiveness is as important in conversation as in bed. In bed or out of bed, most persons never, at any time in their lives, experience a relationship as intimate as this we are living now, in which I express my love to you in a gift and you express your love to me by receiving that gift and embodying it in your own natures. I know of no greater love than deepest sincerity, and no greater gift than understanding, for it is my inner-most treasure that I give to you, and you are complete enough and sensitive enough to do what few women can do—receive that treasure into your minds and hearts as tenderly as it is offered. It is more than mere talking and listening that we are doing here tonight; it is an act of pure affection. We are more naked now than we have ever been. These words are not being born in me because I like to talk; they are being pulled out of me by the thirst that is in you. This is an action in which we all take part. This is a complete relationship. This is the true meaning of integrity."

Silence. Strong's utterance had culminated in an extreme intensity of sincerity which affected them all. Joan was experiencing the same fire she had felt when in his arms, and the other two girls had felt flashes of it. All sat quietly for a few minutes.

"If you can understand the happiness that can come from the mental relationship between man and woman," Strong continued, "you will see that modern civilization places altogether too much emphasis upon woman's body. This is a consequence of the commercial nature of our culture. Woman's body is the bait in nature's cycle of reproduction, the external personification of some of our most deep-rooted instincts. Why not use the same bait then, to make people buy things? There are many good reasons but a commercial civilization does not consider them, and accordingly the theme of sex is rubbed into our minds from the time we are old enough to read until we are too old to listen to the radio. As a result, the two leading citizens of our era are the 'pin-up' girl and her masculine counterpart, the 'wolf'. Is it any wonder that we as a generation are ignorant of the subtler side of sex?

This that I hold here in my lap has the external appearance of a 'pin-up' girl, but there is a difference. Ada is a live woman, responsive as a woman should be, whereas the majority of 'pin-up' girls have the emotional response of a dead mackerel. I know because in my work I am often asked to take an apparently flawless but inanimate female body and equip it with a set of emotions. I will tell you tomorrow about the nature of my work," he said hurriedly, anticipating the question that had already appeared in the eyes of his listeners, "tonight you must sleep. I am going to my room now for a while, and I want you three to go to your own rooms without talking, shut the connecting doors, and go to bed. I will come back in twenty minutes and say good night to each of you. After that, I want you to sleep until I come and wake you in the morning."

Strong lifted Ada in his arms and carried her into her room.

Then he quietly slipped out into the hall and went to his alcove. Some twenty minutes later, clad only in his bathrobe, he stole down the hall and into Joan's room. She was in bed, looking up at him with calm, expectant eyes. Neither spoke. He dropped his robe and slid in beside her, holding her tenderly close to him. In a very few minutes she was nearly asleep. As he gently withdrew from her arms, she gave him a sleepy good-night kiss. He entered Claire's room with his bathrobe neatly tied about him.

He sat on the edge of the bed and talked with her for a bit. He was gentle and affectionate in just such a way as to make her drowsy, and soon, with a sweetheart's parting kiss, he left her.

Strong stood looking down at Ada. She, too, looked up at him with calm, expectant eyes. They did not speak. She made no move when he pulled the covers slowly down over the end of the bed. Her body was alive, a conscious thing. He sat down on the bed beside her and gently kissed her forehead, eyes and face, barely touching her lips. At the same time her body was being touched by his fingers, little, tender, whispering caresses that felt like kisses. She knew that he was implanting gentleness in her, and helping her to experience tranquillity in her body, a thing she had never really known before.

She thought to herself, "See, how he does not concentrate on any part of me. It is as if he were telling me that my fingers or ankles or temples are as beautiful to him as any other part. Feel how calm and tender he is. This man has the power to make me become a she-animal in heat, and look! He gives me something no she-animal could ever know. I am becoming more complete than I have ever been before. How kind he is!"

When Ada had become so tranquil that she was no longer conscious of her body, Strong quietly put the covers over her, kissed her softly, and was gone.

V.

For hours Jedediah Strong had been driving what he called his 'ship' along beside high craggy rocks that looked, for the most part, like clinker, and, in places, like metallic blue glass. The three girls who sat beside him were absorbed in the strangeness of the landscape. They had left the hotel several hours before and were driving along the edge of a weird area of desolation, a sea of frozen waves of black lava. It stretched as far as the eye could see. Suddenly and without warning Strong turned from the road and headed straight for a tangled heap of giant black boulders. The three girls were tense and somewhat frightened at this sudden approach to what seemed to them like another world, and they talked excitedly. As they came closer to the iridescent blue crags, a way suddenly opened and the car sped through a narrow defile into a sagebrush flat completely surrounded by black lava. At the base of a high cinder cone Strong stopped the car and turned off the motor.

"This is our first stopping place," he said.

"The Mountains of the Moon," said Joan, wonderingly.

They all got out and stretched their legs, slowly absorbing the peculiar atmosphere of the place.

"It is like a lost world—like the beginning of time."

"This place frightens me a little," said Claire, "there is something cold and dead about it."

"I like it here," Ada announced. "This is a world without ornament, without pretense—stark, and bare, and honest."

"Does the world we came from seem real now?" Strong asked. "Or has it vanished like a dream?"

"Like a dream," Joan murmured, as if she were intent to catch the spirit of the place, and the others nodded.

"That is why I brought you here," said Strong. "In a place like this our minds are free of past conditioning. Here we can think objectively. This lava has been here like this for more than five thousand years, and since it first cooled it has changed little. Five thousand years from now it will probably be much the same."

"It is as if we had stepped out of time," said Joan. "Only your 'ship' is a sign of the age we came from."

"And even my 'ship' is not as much of a reminder as you might think," replied Strong. "It carries a cargo from many different times and places, and its equipment is all from the future."

"From the future!" Claire exclaimed. "Strong, what do you mean?"

"I will show you," he said, and, in less time than it takes to tell it, he touched a contact on the side of the car, pulled out three beach chairs and set them up for his guests, indicating that they were to sit down.

While the girls were seating themselves, he again touched the car and pulled three plastic disks about ten inches in diameter from the side of the car. These he placed each on the tray arm of a chair. The girls gaped in amazement. Each disk was a transparent plate and cover containing a portion of roast meat and several vegetables, freshly cooked and ready to eat! By the time they had uncovered the plates, Strong had placed tableware, salt, butter, and a glass of milk on each tray-arm. "You may have hot rolls when you are ready for them," he said, and turned to get his dinner, which he ate while sitting on the running board.

"Don't ask for explanations," he went on, "let the food talk."

There was something in the surrounding environment that took the shock out of what Strong had done. After all, they were out of time, now; what could amaze them? It was getting dark, and the black cone above them seemed to project into eternity. The silence about them was so intense that it made a ringing sound.

"Listen to that ringing," said Strong. "It is the sound of silence. We shall be hearing it for weeks."

A sudden idea flashed into his eyes and he put aside his dinner, took some kind of a box from the top of the car, ran, trailing a cable, part way up the cone with it, returned, leaving it there, adjusted something in the front seat of the car, went back to his place and resumed eating.

In a moment there was music, a strange music that began with the very ringing sound of the silence, and then seemed to grow out of the rocks around them and tell a story to the stars, which were just beginning to appear in the sky. Joan recognized it as Borodin's 'Steppes of Central Asia', a work she had long known and loved, but she had never dreamed how beautiful it would sound under the stars in a land of ringing silence.

When the music had faded away in the same way that it had appeared, Strong began to speak,

"I said that I would tell you about my profession. I am an architect; I build persons. Places like this are my laboratories, and the cargo of my 'ship' is my equipment. I do most of my work for people in creative professions who need to know more about their creative capacities and how to develop them. My clients come to me in New York and Hollywood, where I have offices, but I usually bring those who need the most help out here to my laboratories. These clients are usually celebrated people who suffer from the pressure of notoriety and whose personalities are under serious strain. That is why I am so glad that I met the three of you, because you are normal and healthy and just the kind of company I need on my vacation. I think we shall he very happy together."

One of the girls asked Strong how he happened to get into such a profession.

"I once made a journey," he replied, "into a land where the science of human architecture is as highly developed as are the physical sciences in the world we came from. I spent enough time in that land to learn about as much of what passes for knowledge there as a college graduate knows of what passes for knowledge among us. As a result, I can be of as much help to an individual of the world we know as the average college graduate of our people can be to the people among whom I lived and studied, for they know as little of the physical sciences as our people know of human architecture. It is as if I had been transplanted to Earth from another planet; I do not feel superior in any way, but it is nonetheless true that I have learned many things not accessible to other people. Is it not natural, then, that I should make good use of that knowledge?"

There was a pause, and then Joan said, "I have felt from the first that there is something in you that is a kind of moral knowledge and strength. But what led you to search for it? Why did you make the journey of which you speak?"

Strong looked into Joan's guileless eyes exactly as if he were taking a long, refreshing drink of her clear simplicity, and then he answered,

"I don't really know, Joan. Perhaps because I was born into a rich family and wanted to do something to earn what I already had received. Perhaps, because I was extremely unhappy and wanted to look into the reasons for unhappiness. Perhaps because my hobby is mathematical analysis and I naturally gravitated into the study of other forms of analysis. And perhaps for none of these reasons."

He got up and produced a hot roll for each of them. As he sat down again, he said,

"I have promised to teach you all I can. Usually, when I am working with a client, I must carefully plan the sequence of subjects, because the person I am trying to help has a mind full of strain and suspicion. With you that is not necessary, for you are like three bright new pennies,—not yet scarred by the world. Also, you have confidence in me, and are aware that I love you. You yourselves may therefore choose what we shall discuss and when we shall discuss it. You are here for me and I am here for you. I shall most certainly make use of you, so do not hesitate to make use of me."

Strong now began to eat the hot roll, which he had buttered while talking.

"I will make use of you, Strong," Claire said thoughtfully. "I want you to tell us the one thing which it is most important for us to know."

Strong finished his dinner without haste before answering.

"Those who pursue happiness do not find it; happiness comes only to those who stop seeking it."

The three young women received this utterance so respectfully that Strong seemed momentarily overcome by his affection for them. Quickly he walked to each girl and kissed her on the forehead. Then he took the dinner things away and brought three cots from the car. After placing the cots on three sides of his 'ship', he again adjusted something in the front seat, and soon there was more music. It was quite dark now, and the stars overhead were so clear and bright that they did not twinkle. Strong saw to it that the girls were comfortably located, and then, one at a time, he took each for a walk out into the sagebrush and under the still and shining sky.

Joan recognized the music that was floating down from the cone—Rachmaninof's beautiful and tranquil 'Isle of the Dead', Sibelius' 'Swan of Tuonela', and also, when they had been tucked in their cots and kissed good night, the 'Isle of the Dead' again. After that there was silence, and she lay looking at the stars overhead until she fell asleep.

During the night it seemed to Joan that she was climbing, step by step, up to the stars, hand in hand with Jedediah Strong. Soon they reached the stars and continued climbing up through a star-filled universe, whereupon she noticed that she and Strong had become one being, climbing, step by step. Then they were not a climbing being anymore; they were the star-filled universe itself, silently glowing.

Claire dreamed that she and a strange man were standing in front of Strong, who spoke to her, saying, "This is the man you wanted, Claire. He will love you as truly as you love him. He wants one woman only, and you are she. If you are wise, you will be happy together."

Her heart leaped as she heard these words, and she ached with the desire to see the face of the man beside her, but she could not turn her head. She tried and tried to turn, but it did not seem to be intended in the dream that she should succeed. Finally, exerting all her will, she saw—and the face was that of Jedediah Strong.

Ada did not dream, but before she went to sleep she thought about the man she wanted. She had become aware of something which made her desire for him nearly unbearable. It was the knowledge that nothing could force him to take advantage of her, that he was stronger than his desire. She wanted him so much that it was like pain, but she loved the pain, and felt no impatience. She knew that Strong would delay until he had helped her become wise enough to be fully responsible for her actions—then he would let her decide. As she lay there in the night, the feel of his moral strength was as exciting to her as she felt the strength of his flesh would be later. Ada was learning something few women know—the measure of a man.

The next morning Strong provided each of them with a steam bath in a compartment of 'the ship.' The 'ship' had the external appearance of a fairly large delivery car, with a built-in Pullman-style lavatory, a lower compartment, a sleeping space and many kinds of built-in equipment. It was, indeed, a complete laboratory. He had awakened them with some strange music that seemed to blend with the weird landscape—something by Villa-Lobos, Joan thought.

After a rather miraculous breakfast Strong suggested that they climb to the top of the cinder cone which towered overhead. He cautioned them to proceed carefully, as the lava was brittle and sharp. At the top of the several-hundred foot cone they found an opening five or six feet in diameter which disappeared into blackness.

"Go close to it, and look down in," Strong urged them. "You will receive a surprise"

The three girls cautiously looked down into the blackness. They could not see very far. Suddenly all three of them cried out as if with one voice, "It's cold!" It was true. Air, as cold as ice, came from the cone. Excitedly they besieged Strong for explanations.

"This country is cold in the winter," he said, "and openings like this receive much snow and ice. Some of it lasts all summer. Drop a rock down and you can hear it hit the frozen snow."

They did so, and, sure enough, in a few seconds they heard it strike, but not on rock—a soft thud instead of a crash. Gingerly they picked their way down to the 'ship', and in a few minutes they were off, leaving the Mountains of the Moon and driving toward the south.

This time Strong had arranged for them to listen to music while they were driving.

"There is fire in good music," he said, "and if you absorb a great deal of it, you will become much stronger emotionally."

He told them stories about the music, and the men who wrote it, as they drove along. He did not discuss music as if it were made of notes, but rather as if it were made of thoughts. The girls felt that to him it was a living thing.

As the day went on Joan, Claire and Ada became acquainted with new friends—Bach, Mozart, Beethoven, Chaikovsky, Moussorgsky, Rimsky-Korsakoff, Stravinsky, Villa-Lobos, Lecuona,—and Sibelius. Strong knew them all as well as if he had lived next door to them, and he made them seem real and fresh and exciting. Ada, for example, had always been repelled by Bach; now she discovered that the 'Passacaglia and Fugue in C Minor', could give her shivers of fire.

Strong also read to them—by means of records he had made of things he liked. He introduced them to Walt Whitman through his recordings of 'Crossing Brooklyn Ferry', 'Song of the Rolling Earth', and 'Song of Myself.' He told them stories about Walt and showed them a very handsome picture of him. "If you ever meet a man like that," he said, "follow him until he sets you free. Such a man is a perfect lover and teacher and friend."

Strong's eyes were on the road ahead, so he did not see the secret smiling radiance that appeared for a moment in three pairs of eyes.

VI.

It was after dark when Strong and his three passengers reached their second stopping place. They had left the main road and traveled due South between two high ranges of mountains in sagebrush desert country. The sagebrush seemed to end just below the low rise on which they stopped, and beyond it, on a low level, there extended a mysterious field of silver. Though the unwinking desert stars were bright, they could see no more. Mountains to the East, mountains to the West, sagebrush to the North, and something white and silver to the South—it was like being on another planet. East, West, and North were as silent and motionless as only desert night can he, but that which stretched to the South was like a thing unthought of, like an impossibility seen face to face. No sense of danger came from it—in fact nothing seemed to come from it—yet it awoke in each of them an unimaginable terror.

"We have arrived at the edge of the human mind," said Strong. "When I first saw this, I thought I had gone insane. Even now that I know what it is out there, I am not sure that I know. We often think thoughts for which there are no words; this is an experience for which there are no thoughts. Look at it! It does not threaten or attract. It does nothing, and for some reason our minds cannot take hold of it. Now look away from it! You see? Whether you look or not makes no difference. The fact that I know what you will see out there in the morning doesn't help me at all now. Sometimes I think it is something alive, some kind of intelligence from a distant star. Sometimes I think it is the entrance to another dimension. But how could anyone think what it is? Our minds can't even ask the question—they just say, What is it? What is what? That. What is that? That what? What is it? Over and over and over."

He brought out the chairs and served the girls their dinner. Instead of serving himself, he stood before them drinking in the atmosphere of the place, then, with a wild gleam in his eye, he got down the box with the cable and placed it some distance away.

"We are on the brink of madness," he said, indicating with his arm the mystery which stretched to the southward, "so let us have music to match our surroundings."

He got his dinner and sat down as a weird strain of music came from the box. Joan recognized it as the opening measures of 'Le Sacre du Printemps', but she had never heard it in an uninhibited environment. It was as clear as the stars overhead and loud enough for the mountains to hear. When the drums began booming, the girls found that the insistent beating penetrated their bodies and bones as well as their ears.

It was a strange scene. The light of stars in the desert is as bright as a quarter moon elsewhere, and the four human figures seemed to bathe in the shadowless light. The immensity which surrounded them did not dwarf them—it enlarged them. If they were indeed on the brink of madness, as Strong had called it. It was with the feeling that madness is a necessary part of completeness and cannot he left out. Madness became them.

When the last crash of music had died away into the night, Strong got out the cots, and saw that the girls were comfortable. Then he took them each for a walk down to a lower part of the sage-covered promontory. Here they found a mystery of another kind. In different places in the fragrant sage were round, silent pools of water, varying in diameter from two to thirty feet or more, Some were cool to the touch; others were quietly steaming. Little streams of water ran from the pools on down the slope, but they were so encumbered with heavy meadow grass that they made no noise. As the strollers climbed back to the 'ship'', the pools seemed like round, dark eyes looking up into the sky.

Throughout the night the girls, minds were conscious of the terror to the South. Asleep or awake, it was the same. In the early dawn Strong awakened them and led them silently down to where the mystery began. It was still so dark that at first they could not see what it was, even at close range, except that it was a strange white substance of some kind. Strong walked out into it, and as they followed, it seemed solid and crystalline beneath their feet. Soon their noses told them what it was. It was salt, which in places had been built up into crystal castles more than three feet high. They continued in single file until they had walked several miles into a universe of salt. The dawn was breaking now, and the mountains to the West were tipped with golden rays of sunlight.

"We are standing in the bottom of a forgotten sea," said Strong as he turned and faced them. "There on the mountains you can see where the water once was, about eight hundred feet above our heads. This ancient sea extended for hundreds of miles, and these mountains were islands in it."

The sea of salt in which they stood had now become pale rose in color, and the shadows in it were deepest indigo. As Strong led the way back to the promontory, the beautiful castles of crystal progressed through all colors of the rainbow, and at last became a blinding glare of white.

Instead of proceeding directly to 'the ship', he conducted them to one of the pools they had seen the night before.

"Take off your clothes and swim;" he said, "I will bring towels," and he strode on up the hill.

The pool was delicately colored in the morning light, and before long its color was heightened by the presence of three radiant young bodies disporting themselves in its sparkling depths. In a few moments they looked up and saw Strong standing there watching them, towels under his arm.

"I have seen many clean, and pure, and beautiful sights in my life," he observed, "but never such a one as this. As if I had never thought of it before, it occurs to me at this moment that I love you."

He turned, and in a moment was swimming with them. They swam in every pool that was not too hot to touch, and had a lively time indeed before they dressed and went back to the car for breakfast.

After they had eaten and were on their way again, Ada turned to Strong.

"Strong, tell us about fire," she said. "You have helped us experience it, and you have mentioned it now and then, but just what is it?"

"Fire is the pure essence of emotion," Strong replied. "Everyone who pursues pleasure or seeks happiness is trying to attain fire, usually, however, in ways that are not effective. Just now, when I stood looking at the three of you in the pool, I was experiencing fire. Have you ever, in a moment of great happiness, felt little shivers of ecstasy run up and down your spine? That is a form of fire. There are several kinds of fire; one kind is the most intense physical pleasure that it is possible to experience, another kind is the greatest happiness, and still another kind is the perfection of poised neutral feeling. It takes energy to experience fire, and most people do experience it because they never save up enough energy. Do you remember that, on the night we first met, I told you I had treated you in a certain way because of a reason which had not been stated? Fire was the reason. Many women go through their entire lives without ever experiencing fire. I saw that the three of you had not wasted your energy and could experience it; therefore I treated you as I did. If you had been devoid of fire, any action would have frightened, embarrassed, and humiliated you and of course I would not have acted in that way. I did what I did because I wanted you to experience fire at least once in your lives, and that is why I ran the risk of offending you.

Non-indulgence is the path that leads to fire; it is by giving up the little pleasures that we experience the great ones. People who fritter away their energies in any of a number of ways never experience fire. Talking too much, longing for something, being angry, eating too much, athletic activity, sexual indulgence, too much entertainment, laziness, excitement, and boredom are all ways of expending energy, to say nothing of smoking and drinking. Giving up all such energy expenditures will fill one's life with fire; giving up all but one of them will make that one seem filled with fire. There is in each of us a spring whence comes the possibility of experiencing pleasure and happiness. There is only so much and no more. If we want our lives to be vivid and intense, we must develop the instinct to save energy.

There is one thing about fire which it is very important to remember, and that is that persons who do not have it resent the idea of it and strongly oppose it insofar as they can. The sexual relationship, for example, can be an almost mind-shattering experience for those who are filled with fire (in fact, those who have fire in an extremely high degree cannot bear such a relationship and do not indulge in it). On the other hand, to persons devoid of fire sexual intimacy is like a mechanical connection between a clockwork man and a clockwork woman, and such people cannot abide the thought that, what to them is all but meaningless, can be as exciting to others as an earthquake. If you have experiences of fire, take my advice and do not speak of them to those who have wasted their energies. Back in my alcove at the hotel, do you remember how Joan described the experience she had had? It may seem incredible to you, but most people simply will not believe that such a thing is possible.

Fire is one of the things that you must learn to cultivate, for it will not only keep you in the best of health and well-being, but it will increase your natural beauty. Fire and understanding are the two most important things in life. With understanding you can cut off and destroy the habits which waste your energy, and with fire you can obtain the highest happiness."

The girls were silent as they thought over what had been said, and then Joan spoke.

"Now tell us about understanding, please," she said. "Fire seems to me to be something about which there can he no doubt, like being struck by lightning. But understanding is something deep and subtle, isn't it?"

"Yes, Joan, it is," Strong answered. "I will tell you about it a little at a time, so that it will be easy for you. But there are also many things to he learned about fire, for lack of knowledge about fire is a principal cause of unhappiness. Almost all marriages go wrong because of lack of fire.

The beginning of understanding is the realization that much is to be gained through keeping one's ears open; the final result of understanding is the state of being one for whom there are no barriers."

After a few moments, Claire asked,

"Strong, how does lack of fire spoil a marriage?"

"In the same way that it spoils almost anything else, Claire. Take, for example, two young people who get married. We will assume that up to the time of their marriage they have not wasted much energy, so that part of what they feel for each other is fire. They feel a physical and emotional attraction for each other which is radiant and perfect. Then they go on what is called a 'honeymoon', during which time they run away from the pressure of the world and concentrate upon each other. Because there is fire in it, their 'honeymoon' is a beautiful experience for them, and they look forward to a happy and intelligent life together. But the pressure of the world begins to work upon them, and they begin to waste their energies. Soon their fire is gone, and the relationship which was once a joyous way of living becomes a dreary burden. Why? Because without fire there is no pleasure, no happiness. First, the happiness of their mental relationship disappears, so they seek to recapture it by overworking their physical relationship. Then even the pleasure of that is gone, and marriage becomes a common conversational complaint among groups of men and groups of women. As the saying is, 'the honeymoon is over'.

Perhaps I should make more clear what I mean by 'the pressure of the world'. The world is always exerting pressure upon us to do what it, the world, wishes. And what is it that the world wants? It wants us to be good customers. It wants us to make a lot of money and spend even more than we make. It wants us to eat a lot, drink a lot, smoke a lot, wear a lot, patronize specialists of all kinds, contribute our time and money to thousands of different activities, and dissipate our energies in every way we can, for all these things are profitable to the world. In essence, the world wants us to dissipate, and, to the extent that we dissipate, we are slaves of the world. The world is like a leech that will suck our blood and life away, if we let it. It is the world that steals our fire, our pleasure and happiness, if we yield to it."

Strong reached down and turned on the music mechanism.

"We are on a vacation from the world," he said. "Let's not talk about it any more."

They listened to the music for many miles, discovering, as they listened, that even musical utterances by creative persons seem to speak of fire and understanding. Almost everywhere on the mountain sides they could see the beaches of the forgotten sea. The country was all mountains and sagebrush stretching away into the distance. Along toward evening they drove through an inconspicuous cut in a low, rolling hill and were confronted with a sight not likely to be forgotten. Each of the girls cried out in spontaneous joy and admiration.

Straight ahead of them, and to the distant right and left, there lay a vast, sparkling sea of sapphire blue water. It was surrounded by high desert mountains and bathed in such clear air that it seemed to fill the entire countryside with radiant life. The young women had never seen anything more beautiful, and the sudden shock of it left them speechless after their first outburst. Strong stopped the car and they stood beside it enjoying the view.

"This is the last of the forgotten sea," he said, "and the Water People call it by the name of the ancient fish which still survives in these waters. We have arrived at our destination."

VII.

After drinking in the view for a few minutes, Jedediah Strong and his three guests climbed into their car and drove along the mountainside overlooking the beautiful desert sea. Soon they came to a small settlement among tall cottonwood trees. Strong drove through the settlement to a little house beyond it, and there he stopped. An Indian and a gentle old black man, both in blue jeans and shirts to match, came out to meet them.

"Hello, Jim! Hello, Harvey! Did you get a telegram from me?" Strong sang out, like an irresponsible boy coming home.

"The telegram come in the mail this morning'," said the old man, smiling. "It like to not got here."

"'The boat's all set to go when you guys is ready," the Indian added.

"Us guys'll be ready in fifteen minutes, chief," answered Strong, laughing. "We'll be down by the time you have the baggage loaded. What do you think of the souvenirs I've collected, gentlemen? Joan, Claire, and Ada, this is Jim, who has looked after me all my life, and Harvey, whose great-grandfather was the wise leader of the Water People, and who is himself the grand admiral of our local navy."

The girls shook hands with Jim, who said they were "sure pretty souvenirs," and with Harvey, who drove off in the car to load the boat.

"Go inside and make yourselves more beautiful (if possible) while Jim gives me all the local gossip," said Strong, showing them into the house.

As they washed away the dryness of their skins, they could hear the old negro laughing and talking with the irrepressible Strong.

It was more than a thousand feet to the shore, and Jim and his four visitors walked more than half of the distance before they could see Harvey and the small cabin cruiser known locally as the 'navy'.

In a few moments they were on their way, waving to Jim on the pier as he dwindled into the distance. It was a lovely trip. The mountains and sky were colored as only the desert sunset can color them, and the water was fragrant and fresh in their faces when they hung over the side. Strong sat with them in the back of the boat and told them about Harvey.

"You heard what he called us when we arrived? Well, Harvey has had a college education and can speak excellent English, but he prefers his own manner of speech. Many years ago a President of the United States came here, with some senators and cabinet members, to go fishing. They made arrangements to employ Harvey and his boat, and asked him how soon the trip might start. Whenever you guys is ready, he told them.

Harvey's great-grandfather was a remarkable man, Strong went on, and there are old ones still living who knew him well, but, for the most part, the descendants of the Water People are not the men and women their forebears were. The glittering falseness and power of the white man's civilization has destroyed their faith in the sources of their strength, and now all too many of them are imitation white men, so to speak."

The boat was now several miles from the nearest shore, and the immensity of the desert sea began to make itself felt. Though Strong had said the mountains rose a mile above the water, they now seemed to be low-lying hills of no great elevation. Here and there curious rock formations rose above the waves, and high overhead giant white birds with black-tipped wings circled slowly in the sky. The sun was below the horizon now, but its light still rested on some of the mountains, and the water had become pale lavender in color. Ahead of them they could see a high wall of cliffs perhaps half a mile high, but still far away.

Joan, Claire and Ada were enchanted by their surroundings, each in a different way. Joan seemed poised as if about to float away into the sunset, Claire was absorbed in each and every detail of what she saw, and Ada was letting her body drink in the atmosphere of the place. It appeared that Strong was reacting in all three ways at once, if that were possible. Soon, however, he studied the approaching wall of rock and then turned to them.

"I must tell you where we are going," he said, "and that involves a long story. Do you remember that, when we were in the Mountains of the Moon, I told you I was a mathematician? Well, I have a friend who is also a mathematician, and who has been working on one of the most important of all problems,—to find the most intelligent kind of organization, or government. Some years ago he found what seemed to be a suitable solution, and we are about to visit a community of people who have chosen to live in the way he suggested.

My friend, whose name is Hyatt Mansell, set himself the problem in this way: Given a number of people, how shall their opinions be weighted so as to combine most intelligently? If all opinions are given equal weight, only the average opinion is obtained; if opinions are to be given different weights, who shall say how? Proceeding in a straightforward mathematical manner, Mansell hit upon a workable solution to the problem: *Opinions shall be given different weights, and all shall say how.* I was one of those who made the first test of his method, and although it is not easy to understand, I will try to make it clear to you.

At the start, our opinions were given equal weights, and we took upon ourselves the task of determining which of our group were in the top half. Our individual votes were kept secret; only the totals were compared. When the top half had been selected, their opinions were given double weight, and we all made a second attempt to determine the two halves of our group. This time there was a difference in our selection, because of the differently weighted opinions. Well, we kept on voting and classifying until a point of stability was reached, and the two halves elected the same two halves. That is how we started.

Before long our opinions were weighted according to Mansell's plan: everyone had at least one vote, the top half had two votes apiece, the top third had three votes apiece, the top fourth had four votes apiece, and so on. Since he is more of a cold-blooded mathematician than I am, Mansell was completely indifferent as to who had what ratings, but at my suggestion he arranged things so that those with higher ratings are known to others only as equals. In other words, if you are in the top twentieth of the group and I am in the top fifth, all I can learn about you is that you are in the top fifth, so I regard you as an equal and do not resent you.

The ratings change, of course, like stock prices, and must be continually brought up to date. The whole business is quite complicated—which is probably why it hasn't appeared before—but our experience has shown that it is well worth the trouble. At the present time there are several thousand of us who have taken part in collecting and estimating the ratings of over a hundred thousand people, and this community here is just one of many projects which operate according to Mansell's specifications. You have already seen some of them."

Here Strong paused while the three girls racked their brains in search of projects they had seen, then he continued,

"Remember the house where we met Jim and Harvey? It belonged to me once; now it belongs to a Mansell corporation. Harvey and I used to own this boat; now it, too, belongs to a Mansell corporation. Such a corporation built my 'ship' for me and maintains my offices in New York and Hollywood. Mansell's plan of organization has become an important factor in the life of everyone you have met and will meet here."

"But why should Mansell be so powerful?" Claire wanted to know.

"He sounds like a dictator to me."

"You must tell him that to his face, Claire, if you can," Strong laughed. "He is here, and you will see him soon."

The thought of Mansell as a dictator seemed to amuse him

"You see, no one really controls a Mansell corporation. Such an organization is controlled by the combined intelligence of its members, and Mansell is merely the man who discovered the formula by means of which the combining is done. Many of us believe that his formula will eventually spread all over the world, and we tease him endlessly about it by calling him all sorts of high sounding political names. Actually, his mind doesn't even think in terms of politics; he thinks about numbers, and curves, and spaces, and relations, and operations, in about that order."

"Then why does everyone tease him?" asked Joan.

"Because when we do, he looks at us as if we were stark, staring mad. He doesn't mind it, Joan; his poise is as solid as rock. Hyatt Mansell is about the best friend I have, and well, you'll see him soon and know why."

They were approaching the shore now—a steeply sloping rock wall about three thousand feet high and five or six miles wide. The boat headed for a little delta-like projection of land where a narrow canyon came down through the rock. They lost no time in landing, waved good-bye to Harvey, and, carrying their suitcases, walked into the shadows of the narrow, dark canyon. After rounding a turn they came to the base of a small inclined railway which seemed to go straight up the slope to the sky. Strong loaded them into a little car, climbed in with them, touched a control and up they went. It was an amazing ride. The world dropped away beneath them until even the desert sea began to appear narrow. Strong told them that the incline was nearly four thousand feet high, but it seemed more like four thousand miles. At the top they transferred to another car on a level track, and began to wind slowly up and away from the rock wall. The view was unbelievable.

Not only was the jewel like desert sea, indigo now, spread out below them, but Strong pointed out to them mountains on the skyline that were nearly two hundred miles away! There was apparently one thing clearer than desert air—desert mountain air.

The track ended at the base of a low rock formation of some kind, and a man stood there waiting for them. He fitted so quietly into the background that they had not noticed him at first, and he did not move when they stopped the car. Like a younger and somewhat harder version of Jedediah Strong, he stood there watching them. His eyes were cold and clear, like interstellar space, and through them the girls saw a mind almost as strange as what they had seen the night before. Strong stepped down from the car and turned to them.

"Ladies," he said, "we are in the presence of the Solver of the Problem, the Conqueror of Conflict, and the Bringer of Peace."

The eyes turned toward Strong, and the girls saw in them what they had been told they would see, an incredulous and sardonic amazement that sane persons could behave as Strong was behaving. But the eulogy went on.

"Lift up your hearts and rejoice, for you have seen with your own eyes the Annihilator of Armies, the Antithesis of Antagonism, the Integrator of Intelligence, the Ender of Evil. Give of your sweetness and beauty to the Man Whose Mind Shall Rule the Earth, the First Emperor of the Entire Planet, the Essence of Integrity-Hyatt Mansell, Emperor of All That Are and Are To Be!"

Mansell's unembarrassed and astonished eyes looked at Strong for a minute, and then he said,

"Smith, you sure are a character. The sweetness and beauty, however, I accept."

He smiled and came forward to help them out of the car.

After they had all been introduced, Claire asked Mansell why he had referred to Strong as 'Smith'.

"The earliest white man in this part of the world was a great traveler who bore the name of Jedediah Strong Smith," he replied. "When your friend here abandoned private life and took up his present profession, he stole part of Smith's name. Since Smith died over a hundred years ago and can't defend himself, I occasionally act for him and remind Strong that he'd better be careful what he does with a good man's name."

They all laughed, and Mansell led them up some steps which were cut in a recess of the rock. It was a short climb, and at the top they found themselves on a level terrace which extended ahead of them for several hundred feet.

"You can leave this batch of sweetness and beauty with me," Mansell said to Strong, "you're wanted up ahead."

Ahead of them, at intervals of about a hundred feet, there stood three women. After a quiet glance at each of his companions, Strong walked on along the terrace until he came to the first of the three. The girls watched excitedly, for the women standing before them were internationally famous.

"Those are three of our friend's achievements," Mansell commented. "The qualities which have made them so widely known are due to him. Don't be surprised at the way they greet him, for they love him even as you do. But don't get the impression that Strong's life is just a bed of roses, for he suffers about as much unhappiness as anyone I know."

"Unhappiness!" exclaimed Joan. "But how?"

The thought of Strong experiencing unhappiness aroused her instantly. Mansell turned to her with admiration in his eyes.

"If Strong were unhappy, would you share his unhappiness, every pain, every sorrow—just to help him?" he asked her.

"Yes, yes, of course I would," Joan cried, her eyes blazing. "Every pain, every sorrow—I would take it all, if I could!"

The interstellar clearness of Mansell's eyes had softened a bit when he answered her.

"Then it will be easy for you to understand the nature of Strong's unhappiness, Joan." His voice was gentle, and filled with respect. "You see, what you would like to do for him is what he does for others."

VIII.

Hyatt Mansell and the three girls stood watching Jedediah Strong as he greeted the radio singing star, May Lee. It was a simple greeting, consisting of a long look, a kiss on the forehead, and perhaps a word or two. Then he went on, and Mansell introduced the girls to the beautiful singer. Joan had time to notice that May Lee had fire in her speaking voice, before they all turned to watch Strong greet the second lady, the great screen and stage actress, Elizabeth Fielding. They saw him take her hands in his, talk with her a moment most tenderly, then walk on. Soon, they, too, had met the distinguished actress, and, with her, were watching Strong's third greeting, which this time involved the celebrated beauty, Lilith Reed. 'Sexual dynamite' was what Hollywood called Lilith Reed, and it must have been true, for Strong swept her into a kiss so thorough that it made Ada gasp for breath. Then he introduced them to the famous beauty, and they all proceeded to one end of the terrace, where a table was set for eight.

At each place was a card with a name on it, and the succession of names read, Joan Edmond, Elizabeth Fielding, Ada Hill, Hyatt Mansell, May Lee, Claire King, Lilith Reed and Jedediah Strong (next to Joan). When all were seated, Mansell said,

"How did I do, Strong? I had the pattern prearranged, of course, but the last three cards were marked just now."

The girls had seen Mansell step ahead of the group and write on some of the cards, but they had no idea what that had to do with a 'pattern'.

Strong looked about the table and then grinned at Mansell.

"Hyatt, you old permuter—the only way to improve on this would be to take away the table!"

Mansell laughed and beamed with pride at his accomplishment, but the girls didn't see what it was.

"Strong, explain this 'pattern' business!" Claire demanded.

"This pattern is an arrangement of four kinds of persons," Strong replied. "People are usually dominated by one or more of three basic motives. The first is the desire to achieve strictly personal happiness, without being concerned about the problems of others or about transcending normal personality in any way. The second is the desire to achieve what may be called 'relational' happiness, that is, happiness involving others and their problems and one's self only in relation to them, without being interested in personal or transcendental happiness as such. The third is the desire to achieve that happiness which involves transcending the limitations of normal personality, and which is concerned neither with personal nor with 'relational' happiness. We all have these motives in varying degrees, yet in most of us one is usually dominant.

It has been taught for thousands of years that it is most intelligent to be free of these motives insofar as possible, that is, to cling to none of them and to be indifferent as to which one of the three is momentarily dominant. Persons who have adopted this attitude constitute a fourth type or class. Speaking generally, there are two of each type at this table, and Mansell has arranged them symmetrically so that similar types are facing each other."

"Is there a special reason why I am sitting next to you, Strong?" Joan asked.

"Hyatt, you're the analyst today," said Strong. "You tell them."

Mansell looked slowly around the table before he spoke.

"In the first place, all six of you are here primarily because of your relationship with Strong; my capacity is that of a neutral observer. Therefore you are all placed in relation to him. Persons who seek personal happiness become more and more dependent as time goes on, so I have placed Lilith next to Strong—because she needs him most.

Those who seek relational happiness become neither more nor less dependent; that is why Claire and Elizabeth are equidistant from him. Those who seek transcendental happiness become less and less dependent; therefore May, who needs him least, sits farthest from him."

"But what about Ada?" asked Joan. "She needs him almost as much as any of us, doesn't she."

"Look," said Strong, "it may sound strange, but I need you all as much as you need me. Your lives are bound up with mine, and your incompleteness is mine also. Ada sits where she is because being near to a man who has fire and understanding is good for her, and makes her less dependent upon me. So that is the right place for her."

While Strong was speaking, Hyatt and Ada had exchanged glances, and it was apparent that there was an attraction between them. Two silent young men began serving the dinner, and conversation became general. The girls were interested to observe that the three famous women were as devoted to Strong as they themselves were, but they also noticed that Mansell received his share of respectful and eager attention. After dinner they all climbed up on the rock formation which bordered the terrace, and sat swinging their feet over the edge of the little cliff. The stars were bright overhead, and in the distance appeared the lights of the settlement, where Jim and Harvey lived, on the other side of the desert sea.

"Strong, tell us a story," said Elizabeth Fielding, leaning back and looking at the sky overhead. "Cut your mind loose and let it talk."

The others joined in her request.

They all lay back to look at the stars, and Strong began to speak.

"Very well I cut myself loose from here and now and I transport myself to all times, everywhere. What do I see. I see beings of many varieties, and time, which acts upon them. In all directions, past, present, and future, that is what I see. But wait a moment these beings are of two kinds, as different as night from clay. Most of them are long, dark, wiggling things like spirochetes; a few are round and bright like little stars."

"Strong, what are you talking about'?" asked Claire, bewildered.

"Oh! Excuse me," he said, "I forgot that you people are in one time only, and cannot see what I am describing. The beings which look like spirochetes are those who are rooted in the past and groping into the future, and it is their extent in time that makes them seem long and wiggly like worms or snakes. The other beings, the ones like little stars, are those who shine with the light of understanding who are free of the past, and not anxious about the future. Most of the worm-like beings are in great pain, because they get all tangled up with each other, sometimes in great matted masses like a culture of spirochetes, and these cultures are so tightly strung that the individual worms suffer from the pull and strain. But the star-like beings, because of their shape, never get entangled either with each other or with the worms. Their round, compact bodies can enter and leave a culture without difficulty.

Oh, yes, I notice that some of the worms are shorter than others—in fact, they seem to be growing shorter, rounder, and brighter as if they were turning into little stars. These star-worms are all the time trying to arrange the ordinary worms into some orderly pattern which will free them from pull and strain. In this way great numbers of worms sometimes lie parallel to one another and enjoy comparative comfort. But no! This doesn't solve the problem—oh, my, it makes it much worse! When two cultures of paralleled worms come together, they usually do so at right angles, probably on account of some polarity law, and the result is horrible to see. Untold numbers of struggling spirochetes are ground together and sheared apart in the area of contact, until the two cultures are insulated from each other by an amorphous mass of dead and pulverized worms. Even the round beings disappear in such an area of conflict. I say 'disappear' because the little stars don't seem to die as the worms do. They just 'wink out'; one minute, here—the next minute, gone, as if they were going to some other place. Of course, the only round beings to be found in an area of conflict are just caught there by chance, as paralleled cultures contain no round beings. The little stars can enter or leave an ordinary, tangled culture, but there is no room for them in a paralleled culture, so they either disappear or are ejected when such a culture is formed.

But wait! Here is something new! One of the little star-worms, a very short one, almost a round star, has started something. After making a count of the relative numbers of round beings and worms of different lengths, this particular star-worm has devised a new arrangement of beings, which is neither tangled nor parallel, but spherical like the round beings themselves. In this new kind of culture the central core is a spherical mass of little stars, and these are surrounded by the shortest of the star-worms, all pointing toward the center of the sphere. Surrounding these are the next shortest star-worms, all aligned in the same radial manner, and so on, out to the longest worms. Since the light comes only from the round beings and the shorter star-worms, I can see this spherical culture only because I am within it; other cultures of the spherical-cluster type must be invisible, because their light is concealed within them. Nevertheless, I see the superiority of the inventive star-worm's plan. It is that two or more spherical cultures cannot come together in such a way that their individual worms are at right angles to each other, and thus there is no possibility of any destructive contact between cultures. The problem of conflict has been solved; the destruction of beings can now he ended."

After Strong had finished, Ada said,

"Please identify some of the characters in that story with their local names, so that the meaning will be more clear."

"All right, Ada," he replied. "The beings, of course, are men and women, so far as we are concerned. The round, star-like ones are persons who have achieved the goal of understanding, and the star-worms are persons of understanding who have not yet reached the goal. The rest of us are worms. The light of understanding is fire. A nonregimented society of an indiscriminate democratic or parliamentary type is what is meant by 'a tangled culture of spirochetes' and a regimented or totalitarian society is referred to as 'a culture of paralleled worms'. These two types of culture have been with us since time immemorial, and every organization, business, and governmental structure on the face of the earth is one type or the other or a combination of both. Except one.

If the average person is assigned to the problem of devising a perfect form of organization, he will be stopped before he starts by thoughts like: 'man has searched in vain for thousands of years', 'others have tried, better men than I', 'fools rush in where angels fear to tread' — all the thousands of ideas with which men have for ages excused their fundamental disinclination to think without fear. Once, however, a man tackled the problem as if no one had ever heard of it before. He didn't stop to think beforehand about his chances of success or failure, and he paid no attention to the lame excuses which are the scars of centuries of inconclusiveness. The problem was there, so he tackled it, and because he *really tackled it*, he solved it.

There is a silly story about an American traveling in India, who was shown in a Benares temple crypt a flame supposed to have been burning for thousands of years.

"Is that so?" he said. "Poof! well, the blamed thing's out now."

Our friend here is almost as impudent as that; when confronted by centuries of fear and hopelessness he isn't even aware of them. Nor is this matter of organization his only accomplishment in the face of universal defiance. For three thousand years men have sought a test for large prime numbers, and have always fallen short of achieving it. It may not seem important, but we mathematicians feel that Mansell's test for prime numbers is a greater achievement than anything else he has done. In other things, too, he has gone farther than any man before him—not because he is more brilliant, but because he is less afraid."

Strong's voice had been so meditative that its stopping was hardly noticed. They all lay looking up at the unwinking whiteness of the stars for a moment, and then another voice began to speak. It was Mansell's.

"Now that my disguise has been penetrated, and I stand exposed as a superman," he said in a half-humorous way, "it is only fair that I should do some exposing in turn, so in my capacity as junior member of the Mansell-Strong Mutual Appreciation and Apple-Polishing Society, I have a confession to make. Our friend here has told the story well enough, except that he didn't mention his part in it. You see, when our first trial organization was completed, everything came to a dead stop, and I couldn't understand why. Finally I realized that, although we did have a properly balanced organization controlled by men of the highest integrity and understanding, such men themselves have no need of organization. They are round, star-like beings, wormologically speaking, and no culture-pattern can make them more comfortable than they already are, in a normally tangled culture such as we have in America. They all thought the organization was a good idea, and even went out of their way to encourage me to go on with it, but individually they had no desire to push themselves forward. So there I was; I had a corporation so wise and pure and unselfish that it did nothing about anything. I had made a perfect machine— and couldn't start it!

Our friend here, the translator, started it. What one superman couldn't do, another superman did; thus a super-intelligence came into being."

IX.

"Jedediah Strong and I are supermen," said Hyatt Mansell, "at least we feel like supermen, because we have brought into being something bigger than man. Consider for a moment: A railroad or a battleship is a bigger physical entity than the physical entity of any one man—so is a gang of workmen, because they can combine their separate strengths into a combined strength more powerful than any one of them. Likewise, a corporation can be a financial 'gang' more powerful than any of its stockholders. But who has ever made an organization wiser than any of its members? Strong and I have; *we found out how to add intelligence*, and we have thus brought into existence a new being, greater and wiser-than man. We call it 'the Intelligence' and think of ourselves as its children, because it is superhumanly wise and knows so much more than any one of us can know. Yet Strong and I are actually its parents—isn't that amazing?"

Mansell's voice was like that of a child marveling at the moon.

"When I got to the point where I was stumped, I went to Strong because he knows more about values and meanings and forces than anyone now living, I think. He is a translator, primarily, and delights in learning how to make one age speak to another. He knows almost every system of thought ever put forth by anyone, so I consulted him exactly as I would consult an encyclopaedia. I told him about my beautiful machine that wouldn't work, and he said, 'Of course it won't work. Men of exceptional integrity work only at their particular form of creative expression, and have no desire to push themselves into any organization. But they can *be* pushed, and there are those who will do the pushing.' Naturally I fell all over myself asking, 'Who?' to which he replied, 'Women.'

I don't remember all that we said on that occasion, so I will tell you something of the reasoning back of Strong's statement. As he may have explained to you, women are, in general, more environmental than men. If the world is unsatisfactory, they feel it more than men do, and they will strive more energetically to improve their surroundings. Strong told me that in his work he had discovered what he considered to be the strongest force available in our current civilization—the desire of beautiful women for the company of exceptional men. It seems that the more beautiful a woman is, the more men react to her beauty and become enslaved by it. To such a woman, the majority of men become objects of contempt. But there are some men who are stronger than their reactions to beauty, and who never become enslaved by their desires. For any woman, such men are as rare as her beauty is, and this situation is made worse by the fact that most women have no idea how to look for them. Strong said that beautiful women could be counted upon to make our organization go, and he was right. It seems that Beauty is the mate of Integrity, and the two need each other."

"Would you mind telling us just how women helped to make the organization active?" asked Claire.

"Well, we managed to get a small group of our very best men to come to a meeting," Mansell answered, "and Strong got some of his most beautiful lady clients to come. That is all there was to it. You see, men of integrity ask no favors from anyone, and—they are used to receiving no favors from anyone. They expect nothing, and usually get it. It was therefore a most pleasant surprise for them to find themselves treated with the utmost respect and waited upon hand and foot by beautiful and sensitive women—Elizabeth, here, was one of those at our first meeting. Do you remember how it struck you at the time, Liz?"

"Yes, Hyatt, I do," answered the actress' expressive voice. "Strong had told us women a great deal about the men, and we were in a fever of excitement to see them. He explained to us that men of high integrity do not make advances to women, because they understand how sensitive women are, and do not wish to be a possibly corrupting influence. Needless to say, we women knew no men of this type except Strong himself, and we were intensely curious about them. Well, they far exceeded our expectations. They were scientists, artists, architects, writers, and philosophers, and, because of the stored-up fire within them, they seemed to radiate a subtle aura of clean-cut virility. It gave us a strange feeling to realize that they really had no need of each other; each one was complete, and independent. We understood at a glance why Mansell's corporation had never begun to function, and we also understood something else—that these men, these Strongs and Mansells and their brothers, are extremely important not only to us women, but to the world as a whole. Another thing we could tell, though there was no visible sign, was that they were as delighted with us as we were with them. They were so gentle and grave and polite and sincere. Strong had told us that if we liked them it was up to us to make advances, and he told us just how to do it. It was like meeting men from another planet; we had no idea how to act. Well, a good many of us did make advances as the meetings continued—not always successfully, for some of the men lived only in fire and had no physical interest in women. Even these, however, in their friendship and the influence of their fire and understanding, became very dear to us—and we to them, I think. I met my husband at that first meeting."

"Where is he now, Liz, living out on the rock." asked Strong.

"Yes, he's finishing up a new tone poem, Strong," she replied. "He'll be up here tomorrow."

Then Claire spoke again. "I still don't see how the corporation got under way," she said. "The meetings sound tremendously exciting, but how did they solve the problem?"

"I mentioned that men of integrity expect nothing and usually get it," Mansell resumed. "They have another attitude, a kind of delicate balance in their natures, that saved the day for us. If you do something for such a man, he will return the favor in some way or other. The beautiful women who came to our meetings and gave of their time and attention called forth a response from the men, and the Intelligence began its active life. Strong soon ran out of beautiful clients to add to our group, so he wrote a book which aroused the interest of a great many women in different parts of the country and even abroad. Wherever the women demanded, we established a branch of the Intelligence, and the number of people involved is growing by leaps and bounds. That is the whole story."

They all got back on the terrace, and were about to say good night, when one of the girls had an idea. Calling the others into a group apart from the two men, they talked together for a moment, and then Elizabeth Fielding left the huddle and walked toward Strong and Mansell.

"Hyatt," she said, "earlier this evening you passed judgment upon us, and arranged us in a pattern. Now it's our turn. We have passed judgment on you, and we are going to put you in a pattern. This pattern expresses our relationship to you, and this time Strong is the neutral observer. Strong, go inside!"

With the smile of a man who guesses a secret, Strong left the terrace and entered a door in the rock. May Lee stepped forward, stood quietly in front of Mansell for a moment, then clung to him briefly in a kiss, so filling him with fire that his succeeding experiences were charged for several minutes with a vivid intensity. Then Joan gave him to drink of her gentler fire, and followed May Lee through the door. Elizabeth Fielding kissed Mansell tenderly on the forehead, eyes, and lips, and Claire stood invitingly before him until he bent and kissed her in the same way. Ada waited like a sexual magnet until she had received a kiss appropriate to her nature, and soon only Lilith Reed remained on the terrace with Mansell. The woman with the famous body stood almost timidly before him, and her voice was hushed and eager as she said,

"Hyatt, I want to give you more than a kiss."

"Why, Lilith?" His eyes were as cold as ice.

"Because you are not impressed by what the world thinks of me. To belong to you can be a real thing for me, because you see me as I am, no more, no less. I am selfish, Hyatt. I want you, because you can burn me clean with the coldness of your eyes, because your thoughts are made of steel, and because in being your slave I shall become free!"

There was a sensual impact in the intensity of Lilith's voice, a passionate nakedness and humility as if she were pleading for her life, and yet her speech was restrained and quiet.

A gleam of light from some distant star seemed to illumine Mansell's eyes as he answered her.

"Lilith, your body is beautiful. Your passion is beautiful. Your honesty is beautiful." He paused, and she stood still as stone. Then, suddenly, "I accept you. Go inside and put on what you wear at night. We shall sleep beneath the stars."

As Lilith turned to go, she thought within herself, "Even if he had refused me, it would make no difference; his eyes have stripped me of all pretense, and he has held my heart in the hollow of his hand. How strange and marvelous it is that one look from such a man affects me more than all the actions of other men! Men such as he are masters of beauty—not slaves of it. How fortunate I am that he has mastered me—and accepted me!"

Mansell was still standing on the terrace when she returned to him. She wore the nightdress of her mood—the intimate apparel of a Hindu or Moslem concubine. She neither expected nor received any comment on her appearance, and silently followed as Mansell led her high above the terrace to the summit of the rocks. Here the rock was smooth and level, and from a recess at one side he brought some blankets.

It was a strange relationship. During the entire night no word was spoken. There was a physical mating, yes, but far more than that was the mating of two sensitivities, two personalities, two worlds of experience. On the naked earth, beneath the naked sky, two naked minds were fused in two naked bodies. Action and reaction lost their distinctness and became a flow of the fire of life. Elements of character, normally invariant, became molten in that flame and ran together. Physical identities lost their boundary lines; the man and woman were welded into a single entity with two minds. At last the minds were silent, and the entity slept. Beauty and Integrity were mated.

The gentle heat of the morning sun awakened them. The sky was so clear that its blue was almost black at the zenith, and the mountains still had a rose-tinted air of sleepiness about them. At their feet lay the blue-gold sparkle of the desert sea. When Mansell picked her up, blanket and all, to carry her below, Lilith spoke for the first time.

"Hyatt," she said, "you have given me life."

He kissed her for answer, and took her down to her room. Soon the Sunrise was complete.

An hour or so later Strong awakened his three guests and took them on a tour of the place. They found that all of the buildings were either built to resemble the natural rock or actually cut into the natural rock formations, so that they could not be seen from the air. No openings were visible, and no light was permitted to escape at night. The deception was so perfect that, even when surrounded by buildings, they did not know it until Strong led them inside. Claire asked the reason for all the mystery.

"It is because there is no safety upon the earth nowadays, Claire," he responded. "As long as there are unintelligently organized governments, there will be no safety. It is one of the main problems which confront the Intelligence."

"And what is the Intelligence doing about it?" Ada asked.

"Everything that we who are its brain cells could think of," said Strong. "Most important of all is the fact that the Intelligence is expanding. Secondly, the Intelligence now knows more about atomic and subatomic power than any scientist or group of scientists is likely to know. Thirdly, the problem of making a subatomic force-field armor is almost solved. Fourthly, instruments which will detect and locate sources of atomic and subatomic force are being prepared. Fifthly, a system of espionage has been set up. Sixthly, nations and their ideologies are being carefully studied, so that dangerous elements can be identified. The list goes on and on. We are even working on gravity control, because being able to scoot off into space and hide may be one way out. It's a serious business."

They went down and had a swim in the desert sea that afternoon, in a little cove beneath a high cliff. After dinner that evening a man came and told Strong that the Intelligence requested his presence for questioning.

"Do yon think you can entertain yourselves for an evening?" he asked them. "Mansell will be there, too, or I'd arrange for you to spend the evening with him. Shall I get someone else for you?"

"Strong," said Claire, "according to the pattern Hyatt made, Elizabeth Fielding and I are somewhat alike. Do you think I might learn something if I were to visit with her? Or may I?"

"That's a good idea, Claire," he replied. "Why don't you all do it? If you each go to the lady who sat opposite you, and utter a magic word I will impart to you, she will tell you as much as she can of what she has learned. Will you try it?"

All three agreed, and Strong turned to go.

"Wait!" cried Claire. "What is the magic word?"

Strong laughed, whispered a word to each, lightly kissed them, and was gone.

The magic word was 'Jedediah'.

X.

Joan Edmond knocked at a door, and May Lee opened it.

"Come in, Joan," she said, smiling. "Where are the others?"

"Strong and Mansell were sent for by the Intelligence," Joan replied. "Claire went to see Miss Fielding, and Ada has gone to find Miss Reed. Are you very busy, Miss Lee?"

"Of course not, dear," May Lee said cordially. "Sit down, and please forget my last name."

They sat down facing each other, and tranquillity sprang up between them. They were like sisters, and both knew it.

"Thank you, May," said Joan. "Strong sent me to tell you a magic word—the word 'Jedediah!'"

"I expected it," said May. "We are so much alike, Joan, that I've been hoping he would send you. The magic word means that we shall know each other well, that we shall be added to each other. You shall know my life, and I shall know yours, because between us there can be helpful understanding. Does that meet with your approval, Joan?"

"Yes, May, it does," answered Joan. "Shall I tell my story first?"

"Go right ahead, dear," May replied. "It will help me to know you better."

She leaned back and relaxed into an attitude of quiet receptiveness as Joan told her story. She did not interrupt, but it was apparent that she listened most sympathetically. When Joan had finished, she sat up and said,

"My life would have been a much easier one if I had met a man like Strong when I was your age. When you hear my story, you will know how lucky you are.

My father was a famous musical comedy star, and I was brought up in the world of the theatre. When I was as old as you are now, I earned my living successfully as a singing entertainer, and I have been independent of my father ever since. I have always loved music and enjoyed singing, but in every other department my life went wrong. You see, Joan, I didn't know what I wanted. Like you, I didn't want sensuality, I didn't want romance—I wanted fire, just fire, but I didn't even know what it was. Oh, it seems so criminal to me that a civilization should be ignorant of fire! That is why I spend so much time here, for only the rich can come here—those who are rich in fire and understanding.

I married a man who was romantically in love with me, because I thought I might find release in marriage. I was wrong. Marriage of the right kind has fire in it, and is all very well for those who want it, but I didn't want fire in something (I already had that in my singing)—I wanted fire itself. To be the target of a man's passion meant nothing to me; I wanted passion first hand. But I didn't know what I wanted; all I knew was that I didn't want what I had.

Strong has told me that sensuality enslaves people, romance neither enslaves them nor sets them free, and love sets them free. He says that true love is a transcendental force, and is closely related to fire. Well, it was, for me. I found that loving people gave me access to fire, (though of course I wouldn't have known how to say it then). After my husband and I had separated, I drifted for a while, not knowing what I wanted. Then, while getting my divorce, I met a man who suited my peculiar tastes. He was absolutely devoid of any sensual or romantic appeal, so I seized upon him as an outlet for my love. I threw myself at his feet, and he used me to satisfy his sensual appetites. He was no more to me than someone to love, and since he had no attractive qualities, I knew what I felt was love and not attraction. Strong says I was trying to destroy my body in a way appropriate to my nature, that I wanted to experience the internal happiness of love at the same time that my body was being degraded and ruined, and that my instinct had led me to pick the right man for that purpose.

The man humiliated me publicly many times, and my friends all thought I was so forgiving. I think you can understand, Joan, that I never once forgave him anything, because there was never anything to forgive. In a romantic attachment there can be offense and forgiveness, but not where love is concerned, Love cannot be offended, and where there is no thought of offense, there can be no thought of forgiveness. In the moments my friends thought worst of all, I was experiencing my greatest happiness—saying to myself, 'How perfect a thing love is, for it cannot be offended even by this that is being done to me; how pure and free it is, in the midst of this debasement and degradation.' The more I suffered, the happier I was.

I became pregnant, and the man refused to marry me. My friends tried to beg him to—not knowing that it made no difference to me. They even brought Strong to me, out of the desert where he had been studying. But he was young then, and shy, without the assurance he now has. We had met before, and I was attracted to him, because he seemed to understand suffering. He did what he could for me—he took me to see his desert sea one night, as if it were something which would solve my problem. It almost did, at that. The fire-forces within me were so pent-up that I had an experience which frightened me terribly. It was very dark that night, yet when Strong asked me to get out of the car and look at the water, all I could see was blinding white light! I thought I had gone blind, and begged him to take me back to town. He was gentle and kind, but didn't quite know how to handle me, so he took me back and left me.

There was I, who needed fire and didn't know it, and Strong, who had it but didn't know I needed it. He was living there, with Harvey then—that was before he took up his present work and name—and if I had only stayed with them I might still have my baby. I went away, and my little girl was born, and died. That really hurt, because I realized that my foolish love had brought harm to someone else.

Well, I sank lower and lower in the scale of the world, and my mind did strange things. In the city where I lost my baby, there was a museum of ancient Egyptian relics, and I used to spend my time there, day-dreaming about ancient Egypt. I began to take opium, so that the dreams might be more real. It was not a habit with me just an occasional release. I lived that way, somehow, for several years, before Strong found me.

I was in the museum one day, browsing among the Egyptian things, when two men came in. They stopped at the lacquer case, and I hovered near them to see what they would notice. Then one of them gave utterance to one of my own thoughts.

"See'" he said to his companion, "how bright and new those colors are! They were put there three thousand years ago, and yet they look as if they were finished yesterday."

Without thinking, I answered him, and he turned and looked at me.

"Don't I know you?' he said gently, as if my voice had told him my entire history. I murmured something and started to back away, because I was afraid of people, but suddenly he said,

"You are May Lee."

I knew him then; I stood as if transfixed. The blinding light came back to me, I swayed, and almost fell. He caught me and held me, saying softly,

"It's all right, my dear. I can help you now, and you shall find what you have been seeking."

I was weak and trembling; he carried me to his car, took me to his home, had me put to bed and called a doctor.

A strange thing had happened within me when Strong spoke to me. I was weak and broken, yet I felt that I had reached the end of my journey, that I had come home. Strong was my strength, and I mended daily. Each night he came to me and I slept on his shoulder—as you have, Joan. For a few days, we did not talk, because he wanted me to regain my energy. I was like a starved child, too weak to talk, and he fed me with his presence and the touch of his body.

One night, after perhaps a week, a scar from my past experience made itself felt. I was resting in Strong's arms, like a baby, when I suddenly became aware of the fact that, although I was clad in a nightgown, he was naked. He had been naked every evening, for that matter, but my mind had been tranquil and I had not noticed it. Now, however, my old distrust of sensuality made itself felt. I said nothing, because I loved him just as you do, but I must have made my reaction known in some way, for he read my thought and said,

"There are better things than sensuality, May Lee, but fear of sensuality is not one of them."

Then he took my body, as a pirate captain might take a governor's daughter, and for several weeks I was his woman, owned by him and used by him, until it became a natural thing for me and my sensual scars were healed.

I know now that this was an unusual thing for Strong to do, for he actually indulges less in women than most normal men, because he values fire so much. He told me later that I had received more physical attention from him than any six others, but that I had needed it to heal my scars. However, as soon as my physical balance had been achieved, another trouble started. Because I loved him and because my body had become dependent on him, I began to fall in love with him romantically, and this, too, frightened me. When he sensed it, he said,

"There are better things than romance, May Lee, but fear of romance is not one of them."

Then he took my heart, as a lover woos his lady, until I could think of nothing except the beauty of our relationship. Sensuality faded out of the picture, and was replaced with kisses and caresses.

We were like a honeymoon couple, madly in love, until my scars were healed and I was ready for that which is beyond romance. Strong had made me clean, fresh, and young again.

There came a time when sensuality and romance ceased, as if they had never been. Their place was taken by something strange and beautiful—something difficult to explain. Are you familiar with 'Le Sacre du Printemps'? Well, in a dark room, when I was absolutely naked, Strong played it for me—on my body! He knows every note and shading of most of the music he plays, and while the reproducers filled the air with the wildness of the music, he touched my body with his hands in such a way as to make me feel the music in my flesh. There was nothing personal about it; my nerves were conducted as if they were an orchestra. That night and on many nights following, I learned to hear music with my body as well as with my ears, and I began to feel the strength of fire. I was being taught tangibly that all emotional experiences were within my own person. Soon I had learned to hear music physically and emotionally, as well as mentally, whether Strong were touching me or not, and then he began to tell me what he had learned about fire.

I was a little frightened, at first, at the internal violence involved in living with one's system full of emotional dynamite, but the things that I learned about understanding finally amputated my fears. I was determined to do what I knew in my heart I had always wanted to do—to live in fire. Strong was not strict with me; he taught me patiently all that I could absorb about understanding and about fire, and when I weakened he held me close to him until my heart was still. He was like an elder brother who gave me his hand as I climbed the mountain of happiness.

Each day I gained more of a foothold in fire. Understanding made me strong enough to stand the strain of ecstasy so intense that it was like being filled with lightning; I began to experience things so violently that my speaking voice sometimes carried fire to others."

"I noticed that when I was introduced to you," Joan interrupted. Your voice made me feel fire then, and I have felt it many times this evening"

"That is not surprising, dear," answered May Lee, "since you have so much fire yourself. It will not be hard for you to live in fire; it will be a beautiful life for you. Even I, who floundered around so long, and got started so late—even I have arrived at a freedom greater than any I ever thought possible.

To tell the world about fire, I sing, and my voice carries fire to those who can feel it. I do nothing for pleasure; pleasure is part of me. I can live in a pitch-black prison cell and experience more pleasure and happiness than I desire. I need no man, no friend, no luxury, and persons with less fire have shown in the past that loss of arms, legs, eyes, and hearing could neither dim their happiness nor mar their pleasure. Having experienced so much that is pure and good and beautiful, I am ready for death or accident at any time; I have had more than my share of life.

I tell you all this, Joan, because I want you to know that what you long for can be achieved; limitations can be made to disappear. There can be an end to fear, an end to striving and longing and wanting, an end to incompleteness. There is a balance beyond conceit and beyond speculation; there is a freedom beyond monotony. There is an experience more real than any others; it can be uttered in four words, and is unreal to all except those who have known it."

"There is no barrier."

XI.

While May Lee and Joan were talking together, Claire went to see Elizabeth Fielding. Elizabeth's husband had gone to the Intelligence, as had Strong and Mansell. After being told the magic word and listening to Claire's account of her experiences, Elizabeth told her story, as follows:

"Until I was seventeen years old, I showed promise of becoming quite beautiful. At that age, however, something happened to me which Strong says is all too common an occurrence. A boy forced himself upon me. I realize now that he was probably trying only to kiss me and hold me in his arms, but I thought he was going to rape me. I broke away and ran to safety. I was white and trembling, more frightened than I had ever been in my life. I cried most of that night, and my flesh seemed to crawl in revulsion. The next day my body was filled with a leaden numbness and I discovered that the presence of men made me sick with loathing. Strong says that my sensuality had gone into reverse, so that the nearness of man caused me to feel fear and alarm, instead of warmth and physical attraction.

That year I began a seven-year contract with a large motion picture corporation. I enjoyed my work, and the men didn't bother me during my first year or so because I was so young. Soon, however, my negative sensuality began to show its effect on my body. My womanly curves began to disappear. I still walked with poise, and I still had a kind of sensitivity and grace in my body— but the curves were vanishing! Strong says that this is the story of almost all girls who would be beautiful if they were not so thin— girls who have more sex appeal in their figures at fifteen than they do at twenty.

Well, as soon as the thinness of my figure began to make itself apparent, two things began to happen. First, I found myself being cast as a delicate, sensitive and well-bred girl, frequently the threatened victim in horror pictures. Secondly, I found that I actually *was* a threatened victim; the more influential and worldly-wise of the studio executives began to lay siege to me—object, seduction. My fear helped me to escape my would-be seducers; I could detect a trap almost before it was prepared. Because I could anticipate a seducer's mind, I thought I understood men. Strong says that these men were attracted to me because I had become a bundle of hyper-sensitive nerves and could therefore be possessed and used (in bed) more intimately than other women. He says that these executives were attracted to my sensitive and undeveloped figure and personality because they had found almost *no* sensitivity in women with full-blown bodies. He says there is a reason for that, too, and a reason for the reason.

I became so nervous that a doctor had to keep my thyroid in equilibrium so I could work, Day by day, I began to look more like the inmate of a haunted house. When Strong finally met me I was twenty years old, and probably the world's most nervous virgin. Do you know, Claire, he had diagnosed my condition just by seeing my work in pictures! He can read emotions almost as easily as we read print, and he says he does it by watching people walk and talk. I have sat with him in a theatre and had him describe to me the character of someone I know—someone he hasn't met—just by watching them on the stage or screen.

Strong came to me through a mutual friend, and I went to dinner with him. It was a beautiful experience for me; he told me many things about creativeness, sincerity, integrity and balance. He told me of my troubles, and promised to stand by me until I was free of them all; he said he would keep faith with me, whether I kept faith with him or not. Perhaps he sensed what I would do—I don't know.

Claire, I hurt Strong almost as much as anyone ever has. He came to me to help me, because he saw that I was in great danger, and he promised in all sincerity that he would not desert me. He says he would not have made that promise if he had not felt that I was worth it, and perhaps he was right. For a long time, however, it didn't seem so. I doubted him, nervous virgin that I was; I decided that he was just 'after' me like all the others, and I would not see him anymore.

Sincerity is an opening of the heart. Strong had opened his heart to me, and in my blindness I saw only what I feared. Yet he had taken me into his heart, and now all he could do was worry about me helplessly. You see, he knew I was in great danger of committing what he calls 'moral suicide'—giving myself to the man I loathed most, a thing almost fatal to a woman of nervous temperament. Hyatt told me later that Strong was absolutely miserable during that period, like a man walking around with a knife in his heart. He wrote to me repeatedly and invited me to dine with him, but all to no avail, and finally I left word for him not to communicate with me anymore. Nevertheless, the things he wrote in his letters sank into my heart, to help me when I needed them.

Several months later, the forces within me piled up so strongly that they led me to do just what Strong had feared I would do. I let the man I loathed most take me to his mountain cabin. My nerves had tortured me for months, and I felt that this final torture would bring torture to an end. I can't tell you about what went on in that cabin, Claire, except to say that before it went too far I burst right through a screen door and ran screaming out into the night— as naked as the day I was born. The man came running after me, but he was drunk and kept falling, so I escaped. I screamed and ran until I could do no more of either, and then I fell and sobbed myself to sleep on the pine needles. In a few minutes the cold awoke me, and I ran on, shivering. Finally I came to the next house, where I stole a car and drove home, sneaking in the back way to my bed. The next morning my family called a doctor and I was taken to a hospital, suffering from shock and exposure. Over and over I asked for Strong, until they found him for me and he came to me.

I could see in Strong's eyes that I didn't need to tell him what had happened, but I told him anyway. He sat quietly, holding my hand and stroking my forehead, while I talked. Finally he said,

"Elizabeth, I was with you last night. When you were tortured and screamed, I had to stand by and watch; when you cried yourself to sleep I was there, but I could not help you. These many months this has been going on before my eyes, and I could do nothing!"

I looked at his haggard face and realized that what he said was true; then I knew how much I had hurt him.

"Can you forgive me, Strong?" I asked him, and he said, "No."

"But it is a horrible thing I have done to you!" I cried, completely forgetting my own troubles, "You *must* forgive me"

His eyes were gentle as he looked at me, and then he said,

"I would gladly forgive you if I could, Elizabeth, but forgiveness must be earned, and there is no way in which I can earn it for you."

"Then tell me what I must do, Strong," I pleaded. "No matter what it is, I will do it!"

I would even have gone back to the man in the cabin, if Strong had asked it.

"Elizabeth," he said shyly, "'you must give me what you thought I wanted."

We didn't talk any more after that. He came every day and sat silently, holding my hand, until I was well again. Then I told him I was ready to go with him, and he drove me to the very same cabin I had entered before.

"I rented it when I returned the car," he said.

We had our dinner and sat on the porch afterwards like an old married couple, talking occasionally about the sunset and the trees. My nerves were writhing because of my memories of the place, but I did not let it show, and finally, because I saw he was going to make no move, I told him I was going to bed and went inside. As I lay there waiting for him, in the same bed from which I had fled screaming such a short time before, I thought I would lose my mind.

It was a long time before he came in, but I can assure you I had not fallen asleep. I was still the world's most nervous virgin, but I was being fair with him; I had made myself look as beautiful as I knew how, and I was determined to obey his slightest wish. It may seem strange to you that, feeling as I did about men, I was willing to give myself to Strong. It's hard to say exactly why I did it. My world was a world of fear, and my nerves were like live wires. Perhaps, because I knew Strong had felt some of my suffering, I was less afraid of him than of other men. Perhaps it was because I knew how much I had hurt him, and wanted to make it up to him. Perhaps I loved him deep in my heart, for trying so hard to help me. Perhaps I felt that he understood me, because he had predicted my attempt at 'moral suicide'. I don't really know, I guess.

I was sitting up in bed when he came in, and trembling like a leaf. He paid no attention to me and undressed as methodically as if he were alone. When he turned out the light and climbed into bed beside me I forced myself to be still, but, to my surprise, he turned his back to me and started to go to sleep. At first I sighed with relief, and then I realized that I would not be able to sleep until the matter was settled, so finally I spoke to him.

"Strong," I said, "you need show me no mercy. I am here to give you what I thought you wanted."

He turned over and looked at me.

"You thought I wanted to possess you physically, didn't you?" he inquired, and I nodded.

Then he told me that he accepted possession of me, that I was his, but that my body was too tense with fear to suit his taste.

"You must get used to me," he said.

That first night we slept as if there were a fence down the middle of the bed. Before many nights were past, however, I had discovered that it was nice to curl around him or have him curl around me, spoon-fashion. At no time did he take any steps to increase the intimacy of the situation; he couldn't have been more gentle with a wild deer. Sometimes, in the daytime, he would lie with his head in my lap and I would read to him, and I also learned that his lap was more comfortable than any chair. We went to bed early each night, and read to each other out of a beautiful book about a man called Milarepa—you must read it, Claire.

One day I realized that I was attracted to Strong's body, attracted to the body of a man! I enjoyed being near him and seemed to derive a kind of nourishment from his presence. I was still afraid to have him make love to me, but I began to feel that I might not always be afraid. Strong was in no hurry; he said that, since I had given myself to him, he would make the best possible use of me. When we went back to Hollywood, he had me take an apartment near his office, and he spent most of his nights in my bed for more than a year.

Never too soon, but always at the right time, he became more intimate with my body. He didn't even kiss me until I was on the verge of asking him, and then he kissed my body before he touched my lips and breasts. Before many months had gone by, I understood what he was doing; I was growing curves again! When I was twenty years old, I was all lines and angles; if I have a woman's body today it is because Strong made it with his hands and lips and mind. He made me walk for him, intent upon the thought that only the lower half of my body was visible, or feeling that my breasts were my only eyes. He described my body to me as men see it, and his words were like caresses. We read the novels of Talbot Mundy and L. Adams Beck together, so that my understanding and awareness might develop. He had me read 'Leaves of Grass' and the writings of Krishnamurti to him until sincerity became part of my voice. He made me study the Tao Teh King until I was as subtle as falling mist. Strong brought me to life, Claire.

After eight months of gradually increasing intimacy, I told him I was ready for him to take all of me.

"I'm not going to," he told me.

I was astonished, for he had almost become part of me. I protested, and he said,

"Elizabeth, of your own free will you have given me what you thought I wanted, and that is in itself a wonder and a marvel, Can I do less? You know that in my eyes you are lovely and desirable, and that I love you. If, then, I refuse what you offer, does not that make our relationship a completely miraculous one?"

I had to admit that it did. Later he told me his real reason for refusing me; he saw that I was better suited to one man only, that I was primarily a seeker of 'relational' happiness. I accepted his decision because I loved him and had faith in his understanding. He had helped me become a complete woman; what more could I ask?

I look back on my year with Strong as a thing incredible. I was born in that relationship, I spent more than a hundred nights in his arms, loving him and being loved by him, and yet at the end of it all I was still technically, physically, and even morally a virgin. I say 'morally' because I discovered after my marriage that Strong had in no way trespassed upon the sexual act itself; he had fed my body upon affection and tenderness until it had become complete. He had done nothing to me that was not a necessary part of what I needed. Is it any wonder that I love him, Claire?

Before he turned me loose in the world Strong gave me an education in creativeness. He had me study the Bhagavad Gita and a book called 'God's Angry Man', until I understood what he calls 'the power secret'. We spent some time with 'Jean Christophe' and 'The Fountainhead' so that I could learn to distinguish between creative men and those who oppose them. I mention all these books because they may help you as much as they helped me.

You heard me say last night that I met my husband at the first meeting of the Intelligence. He is a creative man, a composer who asks nothing in life except to work at his music. I love the ground he walks on, and sometimes I think he is pleased with me. This desert paradise is my home when I am not working, and I have the happiness of giving what I earn to the Intelligence, which looks after me. I suppose my life could be more complete than it is, but I'm not curious about how."

XII.

If it could be said that Joan Edmond and May Lee lived in their eyes, and that Claire King and Elizabeth Fielding lived in their faces, then it also could be said that Ada Hill and Lilith Reed lived in their bodies. There have been women like them in every age, usually in high places, because body-centered minds value material power and are not too particular about how they acquire it. It is the common judgment that such women are 'immoral', and, according to the accepted standards of society and law, so they are. But society is a relational institution, and its standards are relational; it cannot, therefore, be permitted to pass moral judgment upon those who seek either 'personal' or transcendental happiness, upon non-relational persons. Only those who subscribe to a standard can be judged thereby, and May Lee and Lilith Reed were among those who do not subscribe to the culture of law and society. Let them be judged by themselves.

"Men have been a part of my life since I was quite young," said Lilith to Ada, "so much so that I can hardly remember when it began. The central fact in my life was that men wanted my body, and I was animal enough to react accordingly. I mastered the art of avoiding undesired consequences at an early age, because I knew that nature plays no favorites. I knew girls who had learned the hard way, and I made good use of what I learned from them. I soon discovered that some men gave me something in return for the use of my body, and I began to discriminate between those who did and those who didn't. This bit of knowledge took me a long way; when I was nineteen I was a 'starlet' in one of the big studios.

I must explain that word. There are girls who are 'starlets' because they are dramatically talented and are being groomed for stardom, there are "starlets" who are not expected to improve but who consistently give a reasonably good dramatic performance, and there are 'starlets' who have little or no dramatic ability, but who are given the salary and title of a 'starlet' because they look like a million dollars and because they 'cooperate'. The members of this last group are sometimes referred to by the studio executives as the 'stable'. I was a 'stable-filly'.

Don't think that I was in any way ashamed of my status as a member of the studio 'stable'. I had no subtlety, I had never used my brains—didn't even know I had any, in fact—and I thought I was sitting on top of the world. My head was filled with nothing but vanity, and the fact that I was the mistress of one important executive after another did nothing but add to that vanity. If I had had a grain of sense in my head, I would have wondered why I was no one's mistress for very long but it never occurred to me.

One day, we girls of the 'stable' were called to one of the stages and lined up for inspection by the talent department. We were each given a scene to do, and afterwards I was asked to come to the talent department offices for an interview. The interview was with Jedediah Strong, and the events which led up to that interview may interest you.

It seems that one of the leading studio executives had gone to Strong to be cured of a tendency to be melancholy. After inquiring into the man's work and finding no cause for depression there, Strong finally asked him about his sex life.

"Hell!" said the executive, "I've got my pick of the whole studio stable!"

But Strong was not convinced.

"Those women have beautiful bodies, I know," he went on, "but do you have the feeling that they really respond to you?"

This hit the studio big shot right between the eyes; he now knew what was depressing him. Strong explained to him that most physically beautiful women have been so warped by the way men react to them that they never learn the subtle response that men need most of all. The executive then asked Strong if he would undertake to train the entire 'stable'.

"No," said Strong, "that would cost you too much, but I'll see what I can do with two or three of them, if you like."

So there I was, a nineteen-year-old 'stable-filly', being interviewed by Jedediah Strong. He asked me a lot of questions about my likes and dislikes, then told me to go to the office of the aforementioned executive. I did so, and received my orders, as follows:

"Until further notice, you will be excused from attendance here at the studio, though your salary will continue. You are to report to the man who sent you here and do whatever he asks you to do. Is that understood?"

Well, I had received orders of a similar nature before, so I was not surprised. I went back to Strong and he asked me to sit down.

Strong wasted no time with me.

"Lilith' he said, "it is my work to help people develop their personalities. I have been called in by the studio to see what possibilities there are in you. You have been given to me outright, so that I may teach you certain things which you do not know. These are your instructions: do everything in your power to attract me, offer me nothing, deny me nothing, tell me no lies, and try to understand me."

I repeated the instructions obediently enough, but I was secretly laughing at him. 'You want just one thing, mister,' I thought to myself, 'and you'll get it, but don't think you can fool *me*.' Oh, I was smart, I was.

He arranged to take me to dinner that night, and I wore one of my best gowns. I noticed that he neither drank nor smoked, and he danced like a man who dances seldom. At the appropriate hour, we went to my apartment, and I put on my most effective negligee. He appraised me with his eyes in a way that made me expect action, talked for a while, said goodnight, and left. 'What goes on?' I said to myself, 'is he shy or something?'

The next night, he took me to a play, a sexy thing written mostly below the belt. 'This ought to warm him up,' I thought. On the way home, he stopped the car and kissed me until *I* was warmed up, but when we got to my apartment it was the same routine as before. 'I don't get it,' I said to myself. 'He's not shy, so what's eating him?'

Well, he kept up the tease technique for about a week, and by that time I was ready to go after him myself. I started to one night, and he said,

"Remember your instructions, Lilith." A couple of nights after that, I dimmed the lights, put on my sexiest nightgown, and sat myself down in his lap. For all the response I got, I might as well have been wearing a diving suit, so the next night I repeated the performance, without the nightgown. I might as well have been a marble statue; he was as cool as one.

I began to notice something: whenever I tried to tempt him, he didn't see it, but, when I wasn't expecting it, I was often the recipient of embraces that left me gasping for breath. I had no doubt that he wanted me, and he had made me want him, but 'what's he trying to do,' I asked myself, 'drive us both crazy?' Then, after two weeks of waiting, things happened.

I had displayed myself to Strong in every kind of attire and in none at all, even trying clothes that concealed my body to see if that would get a rise out of him. I was so preoccupied with this 'now you see me—now you don't' game that I had grown to want him and want him badly. Finally, one night, I sat him comfortably in a chair and went into my bedroom. I took off all my clothes, let down my hair, then went in and stood before him.

"Strong, I don't understand you," I told him. I pointed to my body and said,

"This is eager flesh. Don't you want it?"

Do you know what he did, Ada? He said, 'Yes, Lilith, I want it,' and then he proceeded to tell me why.

As he talked, I began to glow, for he told me of beauty I never knew I had. I had thought I knew what men saw in me, but I was wrong; I had been misinformed. He spoke of my body as if it were a symphony, as if it were perfect in every part. He told me more about my ankles, for example, than I had previously heard or thought about my entire body. I had not imagined that the desire of man for woman could be so great. He told me more about man's craving for woman than most women could imagine. I stopped being 'a woman' as he talked; I became a universe of woman. I have not seen the girl I used to see in my mirror since that night; he touched me with his mind and turned a 'stable-filly' into an elemental force.

When he had finished talking, he came to me and kissed me. I felt that kiss in my toes. Then he carried me in to my bed, undressed, and took me in his arms again. With his hands and arms and lips he told me again, in caresses, what he had already told me in words. At the last possible moment, before I was completely his, he became quite still. I opened my eyes and looked up to see his face there above me.

"Lilith," he said, "have you ever felt a force as strong as this?"

I shook my head; I could not speak.

"Has a man ever wanted you as much as I want you?" he asked, and again I shook my head.

"Then this is my gift to you, Lilith" he said calmly; "I am stronger than my desire. In every man, there is something stronger than desire; in me, it can be dominant. Lie still, and think about it; it is more important for you to know and understand what is stronger than desire, than it is for you to belong to me."

And, do you know, Ada, he stayed where he was, without moving, until we were both cool again, and then he held me in his arms and kissed me.

That experience was the beginning of a new life. I had always taken it for granted that nothing was stronger than the physical attraction between man and woman. Since I had in my body a power of physical attraction, I had always looked upon life as a kind of cash register based upon sex, and my entire psychology was based upon that viewpoint. Strong's treatment of me destroyed that psychology.

He slept with me that night and many nights after that, but there was no sensuality between us. Instead, he concentrated on teaching me something I had never felt—romance. For the first time I knew the meaning of tenderness, the meaning of adoration, the meaning of being in love. A certain part of my nature was starved for romance, and Strong fed me. One day he said,

"Lilith, when thinking of me, have you ever felt an emotion that has nothing to do with sensuality, that cannot be offended, that fears nothing, is neither excited nor bored, that increases your self-respect, and that is filled with understanding?"

I told him that I had, on several occasions, and he said, "Hold on to that feeling; it will make you free. Its right name is 'love', and it is different from wanting me or being in love with me. If you can love me, Lilith, I can give you great happiness."

As I look back on it now, it seems strange that Strong could live in my heart and yet teach me, all at the same time—but that is what he did. Before I met him, I had no idea what it meant to love or be in love, and because sensuality was the dominant force in me, he taught me that last.

It was after he had explained to me the principle of economy that leads to fire, that he took me into the desert with him. I had told him,

"Strong, I love you, and you have given me love. I am in love with you, and you have given me romance. I want you, and you have not taken me. Is it your wish that I remain incomplete?"

He had answered, "No, Lilith, it is not."

He took me to a place which he calls 'the valley of silence', not far from here, a gently sloping area of fragrant sage that is hidden in the top of a mountain range.

It is a place where the perfume of the sagebrush is so strong and the ringing of the silence is so loud that it is difficult to maintain normal consciousness—you keep slipping into a kind of tranquil fire. He spread a blanket on the ground so that I might lie on it and drift away into the stillness of the place as the sunset colors drifted away into darkness. I forgot I had a body; the valley, the silence, the sky and I became one. How long I remained that way I don't know, but after a time my clothes were taken from me and I drifted on, and then, without having known it, I became aware that I was his, that his body and mine were one flesh.

There was no sensuality in the valley that night—just silence, and oneness. No night in my life has affected me so deeply; the experience has never left me. There was nothing more between us until we got back to Hollywood, and then Strong said,

"Now, Lilith, we start as we began."

He took me to dinner and to dance, as before, and I wore the same gown. At the appropriate time we went to my apartment, and I put on the same negligee. His eyes appraised me in a way that led me to expect action and there was action. I learned my last lesson, the lesson of sensuality. In a week I had mastered it, and Strong said,

"Now you are what your appearance leads men to expect. Men will not merely want you for a while—they will be your slaves, Go forth and conquer, Lilith; you shall find that your life is different now."

And my life was different. The men whose slave I had been became my slaves, and because I was now emotionally alive and could act, they made me a star, and I no longer needed to 'cooperate'. In the eyes of Hollywood and New York I am an enchantress, a 'femme fatale', but in reality I am merely an emanation of Strong and men like him. I shine by reflected light; they are the light-makers. I am their slave; in that is my freedom. I could not be what I am, without them."

XIII.

The next morning, Jedediah Strong and his three guests had breakfast together. After he had inquired about their interviews the night before, Joan said,

"Strong, it is time for you to tell us more about understanding."

"All right, Joan," he answered, smiling. "I've already told you the beginning and end of understanding; hear now; the middle! It is the realization that, by knowing the letter of the law, we can complete and transcend the many fires that burn in us.

Understanding can he taught in many ways. There is a way that begins at the beginning and works forward, for those of Ada's disposition. There is a way that begins at the end and works backward, for those of Joan's disposition. There is a way that begins at the middle and works both ways, for those of Claire's disposition. Since I am talking to all three of you at once, I am explaining it in a more general way."

"You know, Strong," said Claire, "when you talk about understanding, it seems as obvious as sunlight. Maybe I'm in too much of a hurry, but I want to know more."

"It so happens, Claire," said Strong, "that what the Intelligence did last night involves much of what you want to know. Would you like to see it?"

The girls said they would, and Strong led them deep within the mountain.

"I would have taken you with me last night," he said as they walked along, "but for the fact that the work of the Intelligence is sometimes secret. It makes no difference, however, because all that the Intelligence does is recorded, and can be reproduced at will. You will see today what you would have seen last night."

Soon they came into a kind of theatre, different from any they had ever seen before. It had a stage and screen, like other theatres, but each seat was enclosed in a separate booth, so that its occupant could not be observed. Strong showed them one of the booths, and they noticed that it contained a telephone hand-set, a pair of spectacles, a comfortable chair, and a small writing desk. The booth was extremely compact, and on the writing desk was a small instrument panel.

"Explain it, Strong!" Ada ordered, and Strong hastened to obey.

"Each booth is occupied by a member of the Intelligence," he said, "and since each member is a part of the Intelligence's brain, we call the booths 'cells'. There are two hundred cells in the brain that you see here, and other brains elsewhere are sometimes connected with it. When the Intelligence goes to work, each cell is occupied by a member who can express his opinion upon a question by turning this pointer to the right or left."

He indicated the instrument panel.

"The pointer is connected with an integrating apparatus in the projection room, and the relative influence of this particular pointer is proportional to the voting power of the member occupying this particular cell. No member knows at any time how another member votes, and, as I said before, no one knows who the most influential voters are, except those members themselves. Any member who has an idea picks up his telephone and tells it to the operator, who flashes it on the screen, without revealing the source, so that all may vote. The results are shown on each member's instrument board. It is interesting to watch the Intelligence 'think', for ideas appear and disappear on that screen just as they do in a human mind. If you will each enter a cell and put on the glasses you see there, I will ask the operator to show us the record of what took place last night."

They took their places in four of the cells, put on the glasses, and Strong telephoned to the projection room. Soon there appeared before them, in true perspective, the images of Strong and Mansell standing on the stage, and behind them, on the screen, a shining white line of writing began to form. The writing said,

"To our father Mansell, we say—" and then the writing stopped and two hundred voices cried "Papa!" The writing then continued, "and to our mother Strong, we say—" and the voices cried, "Mama!"

Mansell and Strong exchanged glances, then said with a smile, "To our child the Intelligence, we say—Baby!" The theatre was filled with laughter.

On the screen, the first writing vanished, and new writing appeared.

"That which seems ridiculous is sometimes the truth. We have asked you here tonight to record some of your thoughts. We will dispense with the screen, because we think you are well enough acquainted to interview each other. It is suggested that the subjects discussed be those which, in your opinion, the Intelligence will find most useful."

In a moment the writing vanished. Obediently, Strong turned to Mansell and began the following interview:

S. What caused you to take up the problem of intelligent government?

M. The study of molecular and atomic structure.

S. Was your work in that field experimental or mathematical?

M. Mathematical.

S. What did your mathematics disclose?

M. The possibility of sub-atomic power.

S, When was this?

M. In 1940.

S. Did you experimentally verify your findings?

M. Yes.

S. Did you build a liberator of sub-atomic energy?

M. I started to build one.

S. What prevented you from completing it?

M. I was afraid.

S. Afraid of what?

M. Sub-atomic energy, in this world.

S. Why should that be feared?

M. I should be afraid to enter a powder magazine with a lighted torch. I should also be afraid to bring sub-atomic power into this world.

S. Why do you say 'this world?'

M. Because in a balanced world, it might be safe.

S. Why did this lead you to take up the problem of intelligent government?

M. The world must be made safe for sub-atomic energy.

S. Why not forget sub-atomic energy completely?

M. If I could discover it, another can.

S. What will happen if sub-atomic energy is discovered and released before the world is intelligently governed?

M. There will be a new nova.

S. Do you mean an exploding star, such as is occasionally seen in the heavens?

M. Yes. The earth will explode, the planets will explode, and the sun will explode.

S. Do you think that the novas we see out in space proceed from a similar cause?

M. It is quite likely. When an unbalanced civilization releases sub-atomic energy, there is a new nova.

S. Then you think there are other civilizations out in space?

M. Why shouldn't there be?

S. Have we any evidence?

M. The nova with which we are threatened is a product of civilization; why not the other novas?

S. Then our civilization is doomed to perish unless it becomes balanced before sub-atomic energy is released?

M. I think so.

S. Have you done any scientific work since you became convinced of this? '

M. No.

S. Why not?

M. Because the problem of intelligent government is a problem of survival; it cannot be deferred.

S. When you began your study of the problem of government, how many forms of organization did you find in the world?

M. Two.

S. What are they?

M. One is parliamentary or corporate democracy, the government of the average man; the other is totalitarianism, the government of one class by another.

S. Are these two forms of organization noticeable in everyday life?

M. Yes. Every corporation is a parliamentary type of organization; every proprietorship is a totalitarian type of organization.

S. Are organizations usually pure types?

M. No, pure types of either kind are rare.

S. How are these two kinds of organization related to the terms 'right' and 'left'?

M. Parliamentary or equalizing organizations are 'left'; totalitarian or unequalizing organizations are 'right'.

S. Since organizations in general are not pure types, how do you classify the elements which go to make up an organization?

M. The instrument of parliamentary procedure is the committee; the instrument of totalitarian procedure is the official.

S. How are the two kinds of organizations related?

M. They feed upon each other. Committees elect officials for the sake of efficiency; officials evoke committees as their opposition. Partisans of the 'left' arise in opposition to partisans of the 'right', and vice versa. The two classes are always breeding each other, and are always in opposition.

S. What is so wrong with parliamentary democracy?

M. Many people think that, with all its defects, the government of the average man is safe. It isn't, in spite of the fact that it is quite inert. You see, the average man is the exact center of the people; he does not progress. Government by the average man is like asking all the paddlers in a war canoe to paddle toward the center of the boat. If it had not been for the stagnant actionlessness of the democratic, nations, the totalitarian nations could not have climbed to power. During the years when effective action could have been taken to prevent the possibility of war, the democratic nations were all busy 'padding toward the middle'. That's all democracy is; it is better than totalitarianism because it is less regimented, but it is not a safe form of government.

S. You have spoken of 'equalizing' and 'unequalizing' forms of government. If both are wrong, how can any government be what it should be?

M. An equalizing government usually comes into being as a protest against oppression on the part of an unequalizing government. Unequalizing governments are based on the idea that a certain class is 'superior' and entitled to govern, and the 'superior' class may be chosen in any one of a number of ways. If an 'unequalizing' form of government can be formed in such a way that its 'superior' class is incapable of oppressing anyone, it will survive. This Intelligence is such an organization.

S. Are there any other questions I should ask?

M. No, you shall answer some now. What is the principal cause of unhappiness in this world?

S. Dissipation.

M. And what is the cause of that?

S. Lack of understanding.

M. What kind of understanding?

S. Understanding that dissipation is the enemy of fire, the enemy of emotional richness, the enemy of physical, emotional, and mental happiness.

M. What kinds of dissipation are opposed to physical happiness?

S. All physical actions which are performed, not because they are necessary, but because they give physical pleasure or a physical 'lift' of some kind. Indulgence in sex, alcohol, and drugs is the cause of most physical unhappiness in this part of the world. If we are going to indulge in sex, let us keep it to a practical minimum, so that it may be as beautiful as possible; whether we indulge in it or not, let us not 'nibble' at it as is the custom at parties and dances and on 'dates'. If sex does not suit us for any one of many reasons, let us live in fire and make constructive use of the strength we gain thereby. And in any case, let us recognize once and for all that alcohol, tobacco, narcotics, and even simple stimulants like coffee cannot give us as much pleasure as is ours if we leave them alone. The same is true of over-eating and athletic activity. It is not necessary for me to give an itemized list of dissipations; all we need remember is that *everything we do for a 'lift' lets us down.*

M. What kinds of dissipation are opposed to emotional happiness?

S. Too much entertainment, too many motion pictures, plays, parties, or dances, too much conversation, letting the radio run, anger, grief, hatred, longing, excitement, boredom, and so on. Some of these emotional leakages are unpleasant and we try to avoid them; others are more dangerous because they are pleasant and we do not try to avoid them.

M. What kinds of dissipation are opposed to mental happiness?

S. Too much reading, newspapers, magazines, puzzles, games, books, too much education, writing, research, intellectual work, and so on. Excessive use of the mind leads to mental unhappiness; excessive 'emoting' leads to emotional unhappiness; excessive physical indulgence leads to physical unhappiness and to poor health. I cannot say too often that by letting go of the lesser things we can catch hold of the greater ones, that by seeking happiness we shall not find it, and that when we stop seeking it, it will appear within us.

M. You mention that too much education is a cause of mental unhappiness. Do you think that most people are over-educated?

S. Yes, I do. It is an evil to be taught many facts, to be given the impression that one is educated, and still remain ignorant of understanding and fire. Understanding should he taught first, fire should be taught second, and only those who have acquired understanding and fire should be permitted to learn anything which could be used to harm others. Only unhappy people are capable of injuring others. The danger in the world today is simply that people who have no idea how to find happiness have been educated to the point where they can destroy others; in a balanced world such a condition would be looked upon as suicidal.

M. Since this condition exists, what do you recommend?

S. I recommend that the Intelligence take steps to see that the understanding of fire is given to every person sufficiently educated to be dangerous, especially in regions of totalitarian culture, and that schools teaching fire and understanding be established throughout the world. I further recommend that those who have mastered understanding and who live in fire be assigned to the task of learning all there is to know about sub-atomic forces and related subjects.

XIV.

No one book could be big enough to tell all the experiences of Joan, Claire, and Ada during their summer with Strong. Part of the time they spent together, visiting various parts of the settlement and making short trips into the Country of the Water People; much of the time they spent apart, following the dictates of their personal interests. They had been accepted as free citizens of the 'community in the sky" as Joan called it, and spent many pleasant hours exploring its mysteries. The people they met made them feel as if they were in another world not individually, but collectively. Each man or woman they encountered was as nice a person as is ordinarily met once in a year; to find hundreds of them living together was an unearthly experience. The level of the normal was much higher than is usual, and this made an impression more profound than did any individual encounter. It was like living in clearer air, though, of course, they *were* living in clearer air.

Joan spent much of her summer visiting with May Lee and others who lived in fire and studied the laws of understanding. She discovered that many of the best sources of information about understanding were to be found only in old and little known languages, and this taught her the importance of being a translator. May Lee introduced her to learned visitors from the Orient who offered to help her in the study of Sanskrit, Pali, and Ancient Chinese, but, to her surprise, each of these gentlemen soon referred her back to Strong. As one of them said,

"Your interest is not in languages themselves, but in particular sources of understanding which happen to appear in certain languages. No one knows more about that subject than your friend Jedediah Strong, so go back to him; he will be pleased that you share his interest."

When Joan told Strong of her wish to study, he was so delighted that he hugged her and kissed her on both cheeks. Soon they were spending several hours a day together, going over old words and their meanings. Strong tried not to show it, but some of the more keen-eyed members of the Intelligence discerned that he was radiantly happy to have Joan with him in his work, and one of them said,

"Look at him! He doesn't think he has a right to so much happiness, so he's trying to keep it a secret. If he doesn't watch out, he'll burst!"

The two translators thought their feelings were hidden, however, even from each other.

During the summer Claire developed an interest in one of the research projects—gravity control. She spent a large part of her time there, and was quite serious in her study of the fundamentals of the subject. The young man in charge of the gravity-control project was so appreciative of her interest that he devoted much of his spare time to Claire, in order that he might give her the benefit of his personal experience in the field, although the textbook prepared by the Intelligence was more than adequate. Of course it is possible that on certain occasions, when the discussions of gravity-control had been more exhaustive than usual, other subjects of a less scientific nature were discussed, and even scientists must relax in an occasional hike, swim, or boat ride. Friends of the young couple suggested privately to them, once or twice, that their interest in each other might be more than academic, but this was denied so hotly that the subject was dropped. Whether academic or not, Claire's summer was a happy one.

On the occasion when Strong took his three guests to see the theatre in which the Intelligence worked, Ada was particularly fascinated by the idea of a brain made of people. Later, when, she was permitted to watch the Intelligence at work, she was even more fascinated.

"It's like being inside someone's mind!" she said to Strong, her eyes shining.

"Ada, would you like to be part of the Intelligence?" he asked her.

"Oh, could I?" she cried. "I can't imagine anything more wonderful!"

And so it was arranged that Ada might occupy one of the 'cells' whenever any were vacant, provided that the session was not a secret one. Since it was seldom that all two hundred cells were in use, this meant for Ada a busy and exciting summer.

"I've never had so much to think about," she told Strong. "I know my voting power is probably the least of the group and most likely has no appreciable effect, but to sit there and think over a question and turn the pointer to my opinion makes me feel that I am a living part of something more than human. To me, it's alive—the Intelligence, I mean—just as the forest is something different from the trees that make it up. I feel that someday mankind will become one great organism in which people are the cells, and the Intelligence will be its brain."

Although Joan worked at translating with Strong, she spent most of her time with May Lee, and it was Ada who took up his spare time. Ada's life was now divided into two passions—her yearning for Strong, and her relationship with the superhuman mind which he and Mansell had brought into being. It was a strange contrast, to desire a man so fiercely with her body at the same time that she was aflame with excitement about a bodiless mind. Her interest in the Intelligence made her more patient with Strong, perhaps because she was now in awe of him. She was no less in awe of Mansell, but did not see much of him that summer, he being occupied with Lilith Reed. Strong did not neglect Ada; he took her boating and swimming and hiking as often as she was free to go. Nor did he neglect her body; at any time of the day or night she could feel in her bones the warm memory of ardent embraces. Yet she was still a reluctant virgin.

On one occasion, when all three girls were spending an afternoon with Strong, Claire asked him to tell about his work in Hollywood and New York.

"All right," he said, "I'll tell you first about the most common complaint of all. This particular problem is presented to me so often that I simply press a button and play a recording of my answer. It happens like this:

Some reasonably attractive girl or woman comes into my office and says substantially this, 'There is something on my mind, Mr. Strong, that I worry about. Whenever a man asks me for a date, he takes me out to dinner and to a show or maybe to dance—then he says 'Well, how about it?' Now if this just happened part of the time, I wouldn't think anything of it—but it happens *all* the time. Now I'm no prude, Mr. Strong, and I'm human just like anybody else—I'll treat the right man as nice as I know how but does it always have to be *that* way? Can't a little friendship or affection enter into it? Is there something wrong with me that makes me attract the wrong kind of man, or aren't there any decent men left anymore? Or am I old-fashioned?' "

"Well, what do you tell them?" demanded Claire, absorbed in the situation.

I say, "You're not disappointed because the men who date you are lacking in brains, or looks, or virility; what's worrying you is that they lack integrity—they're not what they should be, are they? You want them to be men with whom a more complete and balanced relationship is possible. This difficulty is a product of our present culture; you have been led to believe that it is normal for a man to look a girl over and then ask her for a date. Now it may seem strange to you, but men of integrity don't act that way, no matter what people seem to think. This is why they don't: when a man of good character meets a woman who attracts him, he may desire her just as any other man might, but he will not ask her for a date, because he will say to himself, 'This woman attracts me, and perhaps I attract her, but is that good for either of us? We know nothing of each other's interests, and therefore any relationship which could exist between us might be based upon attraction only. Such relationships are not good for anyone. To ask her for a date, then, may lead to something bad for each of us. I must have some other reason for it before I can ask this woman for her company; attraction alone is not enough'.

In other words, men of integrity feel much as you do about dates such as you have been having, and you may take it for granted that a man who asks you for a date, just because he likes your looks, is not a man of integrity. When you accept a date with such a man, you are asking for exactly what you get."

"Well what is a girl to do then," asked Ada, "go around and ask for dates herself?"

"That is exactly what I am usually asked at that point, Ada," Strong smiled, "and I usually stop the record to wait for the question. The answer is not that a girl must ask for dates, but that, if she is seeking something better than usual in relationships with men, she must be willing to learn something about how to approach such a relationship. My record goes on to say that women usually think that men who do not ask them for dates either are not attracted to them or are occupied elsewhere. That is not always true. Among those who do not ask are those with whom the right kind of relationship is possible, and it is necessary to employ special tactics in getting acquainted with them. First, men of integrity usually have a creative interest—some pet idea or invention, an art or philosophy, a recreation or hobby. Talk with such men about the subject in which they are creative. Your interest in the subject must be genuine, or you'll get nowhere. You don't have to know anything about it; creativeness can forgive any amount of ignorance. But you must make your interest real; creativeness never forgives pretense. Become friends with the man in the field of his interest—it will give him happiness, and if you learn to see him in his creative aspect you will admire him endlessly, for creativeness is a life-giving thing. When you have become good friends and have a real interest in common, it is likely that he will take you to dinner, and he may allow attraction to grow between you. If he doesn't, you still have a good friend, and among his acquaintances you may find the right man. Remember that the best men do not behave as people expect them to behave; they listen only to their own considered judgment. Be sincere and affectionate with such a man, and he will be sincere and affectionate with you; if you desire him, it may be necessary for you to tell him so, for he will not take advantage of you. The right kind of man is not easy to find and win, but I think you will find him worth the effort."

"That's beautiful, Strong," said Claire. "It's so reasonable and clear, and seems so true."

"What is beautiful about that, Claire," Strong answered gravely, "is that the problem can be solved. Let me tell you about a problem that I cannot solve, a thing that hurts me as if it were a thorn in my side.

At one time in the Orient there was much talk about the nature of the perfect man and the perfect woman. It is an interesting subject, for perfection has many faces. Some of the founders of religions, and creative artists like da Vinci, Whitman and Sibelius are entitled to be called 'perfect' men. The world has always been hard on them, but, since they were men and not dependent upon the world to the extent that women are, most of them have made their way well enough. The case is different, however, with those entitled to be called 'perfect' women. For a time, in India, such women were called 'lotus women' and given every aid in their development, for they were sought after to rule as queens. There is a considerable literature about the exceptional qualities of the 'lotus woman'. It is said, for example, that such a woman can calm a man's passion when it is aroused, and arouse it when it is calmed,—all with the touch of her body. I know that such a thing can be true, because a most beautiful woman whom I shall not name once offered her naked body to me when I was burning with desire—and the touch of her skin was like cool water, and I was calm, and needed nothing more. It is a power of tranquil fire that enables a woman to do that, and 'lotus women' are said to have that power.

There are 'lotus women' living today, but not many. The finest example that I know of is a beautiful singer, whose voice is said to be the best we have heard in many years. However, she is, of a different race than ours, and it is only by using the eyes of a translator that I can see her beauty as it really is. She is a marvelous person. In our own race such women appear, but the tragedy is that we destroy them. In the first place, our general culture has no subtlety, no knowledge of extraordinary human qualities and their value, so our exceptional women are incomplete in the mental half of their natures. But physically they are perfect, and, given help, they could become completely so. I have seen a skilled horse trainer break down and cry over a thoroughbred horse whose spirit had been broken by improper treatment. Shall I tell you what made me do likewise? I once saw a girl walk into a Hollywood studio— a 'lotus woman'.

She was as straight, and clean, and beautiful as a column of sunlight. The fact that her body was flawless did not impress me; such things are not uncommon in a studio. But she was like a queen—a true queen, and I could tell by her walk that her main possession was her goodness, a goodness born of a clean heart and mind. Without being vain, she knew how beautiful she was, and, like other beautiful women, she had come to the place where her beauty was needed. I saw her again some weeks later, and the sight made me beat my fists against a wall. At that moment, I think I could have killed the man who did it. Her walk was different. The column of sunlight had vanished, and in its place I saw an exceedingly beautiful woman with a naked face and a slight swagger.

With tears in my eyes, I ran up to her, took her by the hand, and said,

'Come with me.'

I took her to my car and drove up into the clear air of the mountains. You think it surprising that she came with me, not knowing me? I had known she would, you see; her spirit had been broken, and she would have gone anywhere with anyone. She sat there beside me in the car like a statue, looking neither to the right or left. She wasn't even sad; she just wasn't there. I drove for hours until we were high above the clouds, and neither of us spoke—I, because I could not speak, and she, because she had nothing to say."

XV.

"I stopped my car at a place overlooking the sea of clouds which hid the city of Hollywood, and turned to the girl at my side. She was about twenty years of age. She did not turn to me; there was nothing in her face for me to see. I said,

'How did it happen?'

She answered, 'I was drugged.'

I said 'Look at me.'

She turned her head, and I wished I hadn't said it. I don't remember all I said to her, but it was something like, 'At this moment you don't care whether you live or die. I do; I saw you before this happened. I am going to help you. I cannot give you back what you were, but I will help you become someone else, someone who can be useful and understanding, and—though you may not think it possible—you shall experience happiness again. You have no will now; will you give yourself to me, until I set you free?'

She answered like an automaton, without expression, 'Yes, I give myself to you, until you set me free.'

Well, I abandoned my work for six weeks and took that girl into the desert with me. She is a famous beauty now—like Lilith Reed—but she is not what she might have been. No matter how carefully one reassembles a torn flower, it is never the same. She is a beautiful woman, but she is not a 'lotus woman'.

There are many girl children born who might grow to be perfect women. The great majority of them are mishandled by men before they reach the age of sixteen; the girl I saw, who had survived to reach the age of twenty, was a great exception. I do not mean to imply that it is the touch of man that spoils a 'lotus woman'; it is the touch of the wrong man. Perfect harmony in a woman calls for perfect harmony in the man who embraces her, and girls who are in perfect balance should never be permitted contact with men who are not. The tragedy of the girl whose story I have told you is that it is a great loss, not only to everyone involved, but to all the world. The man who has destroyed such a treasure has marked himself in a way that only pain can erase, for he is at least subconsciously aware of his offense. The studio which did not provide special attention for an exceptional person has destroyed its greatest resource, for a 'lotus woman' could enchant the hearts of the world for a generation. The world has lost incalculable health and beauty, for we model ourselves and our children and seek our mates according to the ideals personified in our celebrities. This incessant destruction of our finest women is a thing that causes me much pain, yet I cannot think how to stop it; perhaps the Intelligence will find a way."

They were all silent for a few minutes, and then Claire asked,

"Strong, is it because you can read women's emotions that you know when they need help? You seem so sure when you do these things."

"I'm not sure, Claire," Strong replied. "I follow the line of least probable error, and this sometimes leads me into action, for doing nothing is often the greatest error of all. Now and then I make mistakes, and before I changed my name I actually gave up my work because I could not bear to make mistakes. Now, however, I work for the Intelligence, and my employer is concerned with all humanity. I am like a soldier, fighting a war against ignorance and cruelty to bring people and their resources to the aid of the mind that can save the necks of all of us. There is a life and death seriousness in what I do, for this planet is a bomb, and the fuse is lit. I try not to make mistakes, and the fewer I make, the happier I am. If I appear confident and determined, it is the Intelligence that makes me so."

"May I ask how you came to change your name, Strong?" Joan asked.

"Certainly, Joan," he answered. "Persons who take up a religious life usually give up their names because they must leave behind them all things that represent their past life. My reason is a similar one, though few people would say that I lead a life of renunciation. On the contrary, many would think that I lead a very immoral life, so by abandoning the name that connects me with my relatives I spare them the embarrassment of being related to me. That's why I changed my name, though it is true that at twenty-nine I had resolved to go into the desert and spend my life making translations and living in fire. But the Intelligence came into being then and had need of me as a woman-hunter, so I had to give up a life of fire and take up my present work. I still translate when I can, however."

"Why do you call yourself a woman-hunter, Strong?" asked Ada.

"Because women have need of the Intelligence, and the Intelligence has need of them," Strong replied. "The more beautiful a woman is, the stronger are both needs, and since I am skilled in the problems which beset beautiful women, I am frequently instrumental in bringing Beauty and Integrity together"

"What relation can there be between a woman and the Intelligence?" Claire inquired.

"The same as there can be for a man," Strong said. "My income is what the intelligence spends on me, and I have no economic worries of any kind. I have no property of my own to provide for, and when I die the Intelligence itself will carry out whatever personal actions I may leave undone. I do not have to live in this way; the arrangement is entirely voluntary on my part. You see, I trust the Intelligence more than I trust myself, and I know I could not provide for myself half as well as the Intelligence does. Women as well as men are attracted to this way of living because of the security and freedom involved in it. For a woman it means access to a better man or men than she could otherwise find, it means that she and her children will receive the best possible care and education, and it means that she will have security in her old age"

In the textbooks prepared by the Intelligence the girls found answers to many of the questions they might otherwise have asked Strong. These textbooks were not like other books; they had a clear integrity and impersonality which made them seem like the laws of nature. Yet they were in a constant state of flux—each statement in them was accompanied by figures expressing the accumulated and combined opinion of all members of the organization. In other words, each statement was accompanied by a measure of its value. Joan was primarily interested in textbooks about fire and understanding, Claire was absorbed in gravity-control, and Ada concentrated upon Mansell's organizational methods.

One evening, near the end of their vacation, when the four were together again, Claire remembered a subject which Strong had promised to discuss.

"Back in our hotel room in the Park, Strong." she said, "you told us about rape, and how it has contributed to woman's emotional nature. You said that you would tell us later about rape as a factor in every woman's life. Will you tell us now?"

"Now is as good a time as any, Claire," he answered. "It is generally thought that rape is an unpleasant subject to discuss; people would rather not think about it. A woman who is forced, however, has no choice—she *has* to think about it, and it is better that she think about it beforehand. Since rape is a possibility in the life of any normal woman, *all* women should think about it beforehand. And the first thing to think is this: only a very few of the many women who are raped ever tell about it; there is far, far more rape than we ever hear about.

Knowledge about rape may be divided into three parts—how to prevent it, how to endure it, and how to recover from it. It is

122

important for a girl to remember at all times that body-display increases the probability of rape, and that the boy-friend, not a stranger, is the common attacker. Of course, if a girl or woman learns how to approach men of integrity and restricts herself to the company of such men, she may display her body as much as she likes; she is safe. In general, however, women who dress and posture in such a way as to accentuate their sexual magnetism frequently find that the magnet works too well. The possession of fire is a woman's best defense; it gives her a dignity and value that a man instinctively respects, and, if she has tranquil fire, she can calm his desires. Women who have fire instinctively avoid ornamenting themselves; they dress simply, because fire outshines all affectation. If a woman must enhance her appearance, let her strive for an appeal that is romantic rather than sexual—it is safer. And above all, let her avoid the attitude of challenge, for the challenge is likely to be accepted.

If rape takes place, there are three ways to endure it. One is the thought 'this is a male animal demanding of me, a female animal, a simple and animal thing—surely it is safest for me to take part in it.' Another is the thought 'my judgments are all relative; if this were the only man on earth, I would probably be competing for him.'

Last is the thought 'this man is part of life; in being united with him I am being-united with all men—with those I love, with one I love.' These thoughts are important because it is essential that the attacker's consuming passion be completely satisfied, or his left-over energy may express itself in cruelty or violence. A man committing rape is in a dangerous condition of strain; it is safest to give him what he wants. If a woman is cooperative, she will usually be given time to protect herself from possible consequences. Furthermore, a man who has been completely satisfied will sleep the sleep of the dead, and this may increase the possibility of escape. Every woman must learn all about the art of avoiding undesired consequences—unless she wishes to bear the child of rape. There is no excuse for ignorance in this matter; its results may be fatal.

It is not uncommon for women who have been raped to kill themselves or go through years of mental torture in the belief that they have been defiled. It is the belief that defiles, not the rape. The physical consequences of being attacked can all be cured, and when they are cured they are gone. If there are any physical injuries which leave permanent scars, they are no different from scars which may be acquired in many other ways; they do not constitute rape or defilement. If there is a child born of rape, it is the same kind of child that is born in marriage; there is no offense in it. If it is of mixed race, it is a test, true enough, but it is society that is tested, not the mother or child. To believe in defilement is to be defiled, and that is worse than being raped. Physical consequences are physical consequences and nothing more; they have no moral significance. Nor is there any moral significance in being physically forced to do something; it is no more evil than being hit by a car.

Being raped may leave mental and emotional scars in a woman's nature: understanding can remove the mental scars; time can heal all emotional wounds. To be raped is not a loss of virtue. A good woman who has been raped is a good woman who has been raped—not a bad woman. Some girls feel that the loss of their virginity is important, yet the physical loss of virginity is often the result of riding horseback. Virgin or not, a girl is pure if she has fire and understanding—impure if she doesn't have them. I believe that enough understanding and enough fire can even re-create a lotus woman who has been damaged, impossible though that may seem—so great is their power."

In a moment Ada commented, "Strong I like everything you have said—except one statement which confuses me. You say that a girl can endure being raped by thinking that she is being united with the man or men she loves. I cannot see how she can think that."

"Not every girl can think all three of those thoughts, Ada," Strong replied, "but each can think at least one of them, and one is enough. The first thought is easiest for girls like you, the second thought is easiest for girls like Claire, and the third thought is easiest for girls like Joan. Yet many young married women come to me with a problem related to what you have said. They complain that man, as such, simply does not excite them, and so their married life is rather meaningless and dull. I usually set them to work studying the differences between man and woman. Would you like to hear some of those differences?" The three girls nodded affirmatively, so Strong continued.

"The visible accomplishment of sex is the process of reproduction; we shall consider that process only. A woman can be the mother of four children in three years; a man can be the father of a thousand children a year, in the normal way. It takes a woman nine months to give a child a body; it takes a man only a few seconds to give it life. If all women but one were destroyed, the race would be nearly ended; if all men but one were destroyed, all living women could be impregnated with the sperm of that man within one year, and the race would be replenished in a single generation. A woman produces human eggs one by one; a man produces sperm cells by the billion. Woman gives substance and body to the world; man's touch is life itself. The number of children born on a planet depends on the number of mothers but not on the number of men; one man is enough. From any one woman a whole race can spring in thirty or forty generations—given one man. From any one man a billion of children can spring—in one year—given a billion mothers. One man in one lifetime can be the father of an entire race—the father of strong men and beautiful women, the father of men such as you may love. A man carries in his body more sperm cells than there are people on earth, and in one instant can give you millions of them. Each time that a woman gives her body to a man she receives from him enough sperm to populate an entire state. So far as reproducing the species is concerned, without scientific aid a man is equal to more than a thousand women if he is in good health, and with scientific aid he is the equal of several billion women. Women who fully understand this tremendous potency that exists in man are not likely to find him unexciting, and women who realize that every man contains the seed of an entire race can see all men in any one man. These are physical reasons only, Ada; do they make sense to you'?"

"They certainly do," she responded. "From now on all men will look to me as if they had a sign on them saying, 'Danger—High Voltage!' " They all laughed, and then Claire asked,

"What thoughts can help a girl accumulate fire?"

Strong reflected a moment, and then said,

"It is generally thought that exercise is necessary to keep the body in condition. This is not true; fire alone will keep a properly proportioned body in perfect condition. The highest purpose of our body is to be a reservoir of fire; if we remember this, it is easy to accumulate energy. When action confronts you, say to yourself, *'I am a reservoir of fire; should I do this?'* and the problem solves itself. Perfect conduct consists in living so as to accumulate fire, and perfect understanding is the wisdom that makes perfect conduct possible. All the founders of religions taught understanding and fire, for that is all religion is—what a pity that the churches of the world know nothing of it!"

XVI.

The day came when Jedediah Strong and his three guests were journeying back across the sapphire water of the desert sea to the little house where Jim and Harvey lived. It was not a sad journey, for their farewells had included a tacit understanding that they would return. After a brief visit with the gentle old negro and the non-committal Indian, they were on their way in the 'ship' that had brought them there.

This time they followed a different route; Strong took them through a region in which the bed of the forgotten sea was flat and dry. Here the 'ship' became a ship in truth, for it sped on a smooth, white, glass-like surface which extended for many miles, swerving in and out of ancient bays and inlets as a high-speed motorboat might? The mountains which surrounded the level sea-bed were violently colored, and here and there the four travelers stopped to swim in round pools of water such as they had found near the salt desert. It was a pleasant, leisurely trip.

The entertainment with which Strong filled their remaining hours together had its origin in a request made by Ada.

"Strong, Hyatt came to see me a few days ago," she said, "and we had an interesting talk. He said that he had learned that I had been studying his writings on organization, and would I please tell him what I thought of them? I told him I liked them very much, but that I did not understand very clearly the exact meaning of the word "integrity' which is involved in the integrity ratings or voting powers that make up the Intelligence. He said that he didn't either, but that he had a personal definition and a working definition for it, both of which he told me. Then—"

"Tell us, too, Ada," interrupted Claire.

"Well," Ada resumed, "he said that to him a person of integrity is a person who is coherent in time as well as in space, one whose actions are consistent through time, and one whom time never contradicts. That's his personal definition. His working definition is that if everyone votes to determine the voting power of everyone else, the final results are integrity ratings. Then he went on to say that you could make the matter clear by translating from music. Now what did he mean by that, Strong?'

"Yes," added Joan, "how do you translate from music?"

"All arts are languages" Strong replied, "though even among artists themselves, few realize it. The most creative artists have always used their various arts as means of expressing what to them is most important—integrity, the summit of fire and understanding. Each art has its field of expression, and music is perhaps one of the best means of conveying the emotional experiences which lie deep within us. Hyatt suggested that music might make integrity clear to you because integrity is a deep, internal thing.

Though many great men have explained the nature of integrity in words as clear as words can be, the words themselves lose their positive meanings in time and become cold and negative. For example, the word 'Nirvana' originally meant neither more nor less than 'clearness'; now it is thought to mean 'extinction' or 'annihilation'. It naturally follows that an ancient discourse on 'clearness' loses much of its value if the word 'Nirvana' is translated in a negative way, as is usually the case. The emotional mood of such messages is spoiled in mistranslation, and the essential core of meaning is lost.

Music, however, is not so easily disfigured. If the symphonies of a great composer are presented by a sympathetic conductor, they retain their intended moods and effectively convey what they are designed to express. At the present time there is probably no better way to learn the feel of true integrity than to listen to the eight symphonies of Jan Sibelius, for such is their primary message. Would you like me to translate them for you as we listen to them, so that you may understand what they say?"

The girls responded in an enthusiastic affirmative, so Strong continued.

"First of all, you must realize that I am merely suggesting ideas which illustrate the emotional content of Sibelius' work. Whether he thought such things while making his music I cannot say, but his work definitely does suggest to me such illustrations as I will describe to you."

And as they sped on their way through the violently colored country of the forgotten sea, he played for them the eight symphonies and his translation.

"The first movement of the first Sibelius symphony is an announcement of all that is to come. At the beginning, picture an old, old man sitting quietly and softly telling a story. He speaks of creativeness and understanding, and because in his gentleness there is also wisdom, his vision transforms him and he becomes gigantic, standing high over the race of mankind like the sun-touched peaks of the Himalayas. For such is the nature of understanding; it seems simple and unspectacular at first, but it transforms us and makes us grow beyond our wildest dreams. The music goes on to tell of this growth and of the tremendous resources which it reveals in our character,—affection, tenderness, exaltation and integrity. Then, in a passage near the end of the movement, it is shown that this power which comes from within us is something before which all known institutions crumble and melt away as if before a great flood—it is all in the music—and then, after a brief pause, it is shown that this evolution of integrity which begins so inconspicuously will grow and grow until in its gigantic roar of strength its true nature appears—that *it is infinite and irresistible law.*

The second movement tells of gentleness and affection and the strength contained in them, for it is out of such things in us that integrity is made. The third movement is an expression of the vitality and joyfulness that are part of a healthy mind and heart,—more parts of integrity. The fourth and last movement consists of three gigantic tidal waves: first, the freedom and stature of those who are most truly creative; second, the delicious beauty of the things they express and its explosive effect upon others; third, the multitude of those who absorb and embody the utterances of creative persons, thereby becoming creative themselves and containing in their own nature the same three tidal waves as have been described (at the very end of the symphony this can be heard). Such is Sibelius, first expression of integrity—a presentation of the potentialities which lie within us.

The second Symphony is a long look into the world of our emotional nature, wherein we may see the vast oceans of emotional energy which are ours to use if we wish. It is not fitting that I should attempt a more detailed description, for each of you will see that world differently as you listen to the music. This symphony is a mirror of our emotional nature; to the confused it is confusing, while to the unconfused it is clear.

The first movement of Sibelius' third symphony is a portrait of all that is heroic in man—his masculinity, his idealism, his courage, strength and resourcefulness. The second movement tells of all that is beautiful in woman—her femininity, her enchantments, her subtlety, delicacy, and loveliness. The third movement tells of that within us which is beyond man or woman—the longing for freedom, for perfect clearness and understanding. To me, this last movement of Sibelius, third symphony is one of the most exciting of all creative expressions, for it shows how—that which is at first only a vague unrest and discontent inevitably grows until it becomes a compulsion which sweeps everything before it. It. is an explanation of the symphony which follows it.

The fourth symphony of Sibelius is a positive expression of an experience most difficult to describe, an experience so deep, so internal that words have nevcr told it well. It is the stripping away of all non-essential things in order to experience reality—the searching deep down among the causal roots of our nature to find the core of perversity and cut it out. Do you remember my telling you that happiness never comes to those who seek it? Well, the struggle told of in this symphony is the most important struggle of all—finding and destroying the happiness-seeker, for the happiness-seeker is the maker of suffering. What we call our 'personality' must be tracked to its source, and the journey is one which requires great concentration and determination. It is the most terrible and wonderful of all journeys (as the music tells), and when, in the last movement, the seeker of happiness is sought out and slain, it seems as if the entire personality has been destroyed, and the music closes sadly and mournfully. There are many people who cannot remain normally conscious when listening to this symphony under proper conditions in a darkened room, for it speaks directly to levels deep within us. It is perhaps the greatest single musical work ever written, for it expresses what is really inexpressible—the core of integrity.

The Sibelius fifth symphony tells what happens after the happiness-seeker has been slain. Since there is no longer any seeking after happiness, emotional energy begins to accumulate, and the first movement of the symphony tells of the fiery droplets of strength which appear and gradually increase until they become a raging torrent of illimitable power. The strange ending of the first movement illustrates this, for it is suddenly cut off in mid flight just as the sound of the water crashing through a tunnel is suddenly cut off when the tunnel becomes full. After one's nature is full of fire, the torrent of energy makes no disturbance. The power is formless and unharnessed, but silent.

The second movement tells of another power that comes with fire—the power of concentration. It shows how a creative mind can take one idea and use it in endless ways, turning it this way and that, transforming it, and making it a thing of beauty. The music is itself a perfect application of the power, for it is all made of one musical theme. It is one of the finest illustrations of the flexibility of a creative mind. (This power of concentration is also displayed in Sibelius' 'Tapiola' and Bach's 'Passacaglia' and 'Fugue in C Minor', to say nothing of many other famous works.)

The third movement of this fifth symphony is the wedding of the two forces displayed in the first and second movements, the undisciplined fire-force and the controlling power of concentration. Just as a skilled rider can master and put to use the unrestrained energies of a wild horse, in this movement the controlling power of the mind harnesses the flood of fire and forms it into a disciplined expression of strength. It is a difficult struggle, but at its conclusion there is the triumphant realization that emotional energies are conquered forever and made into strong and able servants. This is one of the aspects of freedom.

The Sibelius sixth symphony tells of the things which preoccupy us when we have gotten beyond physical and emotional problems. It is the world of the mind which then attracts our attention, a world of beauty and subtlety and intriguing rhythms and patterns. The mind becomes like a beautiful crystal, and, for a time, we fall in love with it—but only for a time.

The seventh symphony is an expression of what we are like when we have become free, when we have become perfectly clear. It tells what we are like when pride and fear are gone and integrity reigns supreme. We have then become, each of us, an entire universe of storm and grandeur and tranquillity. Some of us think that we can never arrive at such an exalted realization, but we can, and our ability to understand the music is proof of it.

The Sibelius eighth symphony portrays that uncommon one of us who is not only free but breathes freedom to others—one who radiates freedom. Such a person is a rare jewel of integrity, and I do not know of very many who have gone so far. No more perfect clearness could be portrayed in a symphony, and that is why there are no more than eight Sibelius symphonies. The next higher variety of human is an independent creator like Sibelius himself or Leonardo da Vinci or Walt Whitman. To approach the Sibelius ninth symphony, study one of these.

It is hard to conceive the true greatness of the eight Sibelius symphonies; they portray eight out of ten levels of integrity. Sibelius himself is on the ninth level, and only certain of the perfect teachers belong on level ten. I know of six of them. The first was a man called Kapila, who taught a philosophy now known as Sankhya. The second was Krishna, the central teacher of what is now called Hinduism. The third was Lao Tzu, the originator of what is now called Taoism. The fourth was Gotama, who established what is now called Buddhism. The fifth was Yeshua, the originator of what is now called Christianity. The sixth is living now and does not wish to be named—so I do not name him. You notice that I said, 'what is now called Hinduism, Taoism, Buddhism, Christianity' and so on. I say that because the modern teachings which go by these names bear little relation to the original teachings—which is why such works as the Sibelius symphonies are so important"

The time finally came when the three girls parted from Strong and returned to their homes. Strong had promised to visit each of them when he came east to his New York office during the winter, and it was understood that they would in some way arrange to travel west again next summer. On the eastbound train Joan was preoccupied with her texts on understanding and Ada was deeply engrossed in various books bearing upon the Intelligence and Mansell's organizational methods, but Claire sat quietly and seemed lost in thought. She was puzzled. In saying goodbye, Strong had kissed her on the forehead instead of on the lips as he had the others. Why? Could it be that he had read in her what she herself had not known—that she subconsciously wanted him to do what he had done? And if she had not wanted Strong to kiss her lips, for whom was she saving them? It would take time, but Claire was beginning to realize what the others had known for many days.

XVII.

STRONG—

It has been interesting to look at the world through the eyes you opened. I see two things with increasing clearness. One is that people ruin their lives and the effectiveness of their work simply because they lack understanding. The other is that understanding alone will make all things right for them. I want to learn all I can about understanding and fire, so that I may be of some use. Do you think that I could be of any help to you in your work, Strong? I want so much to take an active part in what you are doing until I have absorbed all I can digest. Is there any kind of work I could do there to earn my keep? I don't care what it is—I will wash dishes or make beds or even scrub floors, if I can only continue to study with you as we did this summer.

As you suggested, I have been trying to decide which sources to study first. Acquaintance with you and Hyatt has convinced me that effective action in the world calls for a reasonably clear conception of the physical sciences, so I am trying to learn to understand numbers intelligently and have been going over my notes on the Sankhya physics of Kapila. The Charles Fort book you gave me certainly expresses the Sankhya viewpoint—no wonder you spoke of the two as related. McVicar's 'Sketch of a Philosophy', is in the Public Library but I don't think I'd better tackle it just yet.

Though I'm very fond of Krishna, Lao Tzu and Yeshua (the Nazarene was a beautiful book), I think I'd better concentrate on Kapila and Gotama for a while. They are so precise and scientific that understanding them should help me understand the others. I want to learn all these things from the ground up, so that I shall be able to explain them intelligently. The world is so much in need of the things that you and Hyatt have learned—so much in need of the Intelligence and all it stands for—that I could not excuse myself if I did not help. I want to really help, Strong, not just try to help.

You and Hyatt have given me great faith in the human race. Do you still expect to come east soon? If you do, there is something I want to ask you. I know you are probably terribly busy when you come to New York, but I won't take more than a few minutes of your time. I'm glad I know you, Strong.

JOAN

Pah-nee-doq, Nevada
November 2

JOAN——

Do you realize how few people in the world share the interest that you and I have in translating ancient and obsolete languages with particular reference to understanding? You are the only one I know, not counting myself. I have wanted a colleague for a long time, and would have put up with a terrible-tempered monster of a collaborator if I had to. And you ask for the job—you who are beautiful to look at, beautiful to know, and as wise as any girl I have met. Joan, I will wash dishes to have *you* work with *me*.

Of course you may come—the Intelligence has need of the things we can translate. I will be in New York on the 9th and can see you any day you are free. Just call my secretary at the hotel and pick your time. We will talk over all the details then. And as for whatever you want to ask me about, if it is something that I can do, consider it done. Whatever you want from me is yours, Joan. Your taste exactly matches mine in the choice of sources to study first. Perhaps we shall translate them first. What there is of Kapila's Sankhya is very brief, but there is a great deal to be translated in the Pali of Gotama. At any rate, the most precise use of words is to be found in the teachings of these two gentlemen, and familiarity with them will help us with the others. I told Hyatt about your determination to get a living grasp of mathematics, and he and I both will be glad to help you.

I'm glad I know you, too. Very glad.

STRONG

"Mr Strong is waiting for you, Miss Edmond," said the dark-haired secretary, a graceful but efficient-looking girl. Joan walked through a door and straight into the arms of Jedediah Strong. They did not kiss, but clung to each other silently for a few seconds.

Then softly, in her ear, Strong said, "Hello, Joan."

"Hello."

Joan's voice was low, but in some way it conveyed a slight sense of strain, a touch of hesitancy. As if sensing that she wished to tell him something not easy to tell, he took her to a couch, sat down with her, and put her head on his shoulder, so that she was too close to feel the barrier of separateness. Then he said,

"Now, tell me."

"Strong, I want three things."

She was calm now, relaxed against his arm and shoulder.

"I want most of all to translate and learn understanding and work with you."

"Joan, as long as I am a translator, you may do that," he replied.

She was silent a minute in her happiness, which she radiated without moving. Then she said,

"I am not particularly interested in sensuality or romance, I want to live in fire."

"I will help you in every way Joan," he replied.

Again she was silent, but this time for so long that he finally said,

"Tell me, dear."

Finally she spoke.

"This is the hard part, Strong. It is my least important wish, and yet I am afraid it might spoil the first wish. Before I tell you what it is, let me say that if you think it will spoil or shorten our working relationship, I will forget I ever had the idea."

"Go on, Joan," he urged. "I don't think you are capable of wanting anything that could spoil our relationship."

"I hope you're right," she sighed. "Well, this is it. So that my understanding will he complete, I want to experience sensuality and romance before I begin to live in fire. I want you to teach my body all that a woman's body should know and teach my heart all that a woman's heart should know. I realize that some other man could do that, but for me there is no other man, Strong. I don't have to tell you that I love you, for you know it. But I must tell you that, though I do not attach lasting importance to such things, I am in love with you and I want you. I can put these feelings away if you wish me to, Strong, or if I don't please you, but—".

"Don't please me!" Strong exclaimed. " Joan, Joan, don't ever think such a thought! No one has ever pleased me as you please me. Let me think a moment,—I think I have something to tell *you*."

Joan was silent, but her silence filled the room with light. She knew now that she was not only loved but desired and adored, and she had the feeling that whether her third wish was fulfilled or not, it would not endanger the perfection of their relationship.

In a moment Strong began to speak.

"There are some things which I must tell you, Joan, so that you will understand my reaction to your third wish. You know that when I was twenty-nine I changed my name, but you must also know that before that time I was married twice and have two children. I could not understand why my marriages failed, and, when I found out, I planned to translate and live in fire for the rest of my life. The Intelligence had need of me, however, so I changed my name and took up my present work. Now let me tell you the why of all this. There is in me a power of affection many times stronger than normal. It is so intense that it blinded two otherwise intelligent women into thinking that I was ideally suited to them, and its reflection from them blinded me. Today those two women are my good friends, which is all they ever should have been, but it took each of them three years to discover it. I looked after each of them until they found the husbands to whom they were really suited, and was a good father in the meantime, but I was nonetheless responsible for a four year detour in the life of the first and a five year detour in the life of the second. I resolved that I would never again be the cause of such a mistake. I made an inventory of my essential characteristics and resolved never to turn the force of my affection loose on any woman again unless she had those same characteristics. You have them, Joan. You want to translate in the same way that I do, you want to live in fire before long, and you also have a power of affection. Yet I have a job to do for the Intelligence. It is my power of affection that enables me to help the men and women who come to me. It is because I am sincere and affectionate with them that they respond to my help.

I have tried to keep my love for you a secret, because I did not want to influence you in any way. I have deliberately avoided thinking about you, because I was afraid that the thought of you would grow like a prairie fire and blind us both. I am still talking to you without thinking too much about you. Joan, if you want a man who has as his clients some of the most beautiful and famous women in the world, who is sometimes of necessity intimate with one or more of them, and who frankly admits that he enjoys it as much as any man might—if you want such a man as that, I am ready to discuss your third wish."

"I considered all that before I made the wish, Strong," Joan said softly. "If my love for you were possessive, it would not be love, but possessiveness. I will have nothing to do with possessiveness.'

Strong sighed.

"That was my last effort to discourage you, Joan. I have held out as long as I can. Now let me tell you *my* wishes. I want you beside me the rest of my life, so that we can work together. I want to devote a year of my life to you, to take you to South America and to the Orient, as my wife, Joan. I think at the end of that year you will be living in fire and I will return to my work until I can leave it and live in fire too.

I love you, Joan. I have tried to look at you critically but I can't. I of all people should know better, but I cannot get over the obsession that you are the most beautiful woman alive. My first wife is the most intelligent woman I ever met, but you are the wisest. I do have sense enough to know that it is your wisdom that makes you so beautiful, and that means that for me you will always be beauty itself. Understanding such as you have is permanent, and will never fade. I can tell that in a hundred ways—in the way you hold your head, in the way you walk, in the gentleness of your voice—."

He got down on the floor at her feet and sat looking up into her face. Joan was still, as still as if she were not really there, but her eyes were like stars. She understood now what he meant by his 'power of affection'—he was in the grip of sincerity so intense that he was almost trembling, and, from the touch of his hands on her feet and ankles, fire was streaming all over her body. There was fire in his voice as he went on.

"I can let all this out to you because it is more fire than words, and fire is your natural language. I cannot explain it, Joan, but the light in you reduces me to complete incoherence—I could not be more excited if you were made out of liquid lightning. Perhaps you are hearing what I am saying; I am not—it is this *river* of what I *feel*."

He went on talking, but Joan heard no more words, for she was aware of a tremendous flowing force pouring into her by means of his voice but not contained in what he was saying. It was a torrent of affection or love-fire or something, and it seemed as if the many months they had loved each other were being lived in just a few seconds. She knew she would never be able to doubt his love for her, and she was amazed at her own ability to drink in and absorb the intensity that Strong was radiating into her. And how was it that she understood so simply and completely just what was happening? She made an effort to hear his voice again and finally the words appeared like writing in a confined space; they were saying,

"Romance and sensuality—what do they mean? How can they compare with love itself? Perhaps they mean something; I don't know. One thing I know; you are my beloved. You are more real than anything else. You are what I want the world to be. You are spontaneous, independent, unaffected and unposed. Forgive me, Joan; I didn't mean to talk like this. It's just that I've waited so long to tell you that I love you."

He put his arm across her knees and his head upon his arm. Her fingers touched the back of his neck.

XVIII.

The Intelligence had decided that the art of gravity-control was to be kept secret, so Claire and her young man had to carry on their correspondence without discussing the subject. Since they had parted, both had become aware that their interest in each other was more than academic. It was not long before the young superintendent of gravity-control found it necessary to make a trip to the east coast in order to personally select some laboratory equipment, and it so happened that the manufacturer he came to see was located not far from the town in which Claire lived. When they met, gravity-control was not discussed, and it was not long before Claire's father spent some time in his study with a young visitor from the west. The engagement was approved, and, before many weeks had passed Mr. & Mrs. King announced the marriage of their daughter Claire to the distinguished young research scientist from Nevada.

When she went through New York on her honeymoon, Claire left her husband long enough to have a long talk with Jedediah Strong in his office. After they had exchanged greetings and congratulations, for Strong and Joan were about to be married and leave on their honeymoon, she said,

"Strong, I am a bride now—a bride of three days. I don't need to tell you that I love my husband, for you knew it before I did. Yet love isn't everything; I need advice. You must tell me how to be as good a bride as my husband deserves. Will you tell me now?"

Strong took her hand and smiled at her.

"Yes, Claire, I will tell you as much as you need to know now. If you ever need to know more, I will tell you when you need it.

Your marriage will be complete if it contains sensuality, romance, and love. I can tell by looking at you that you have all three at present, so what I say is merely to help you keep them. You have the feeling that your body is your husband's property.

Keep that feeling; it is the basis of sensual response. Physically you must be your husband's slave, as submissive and responsive as a willing slave-girl. When women forget this, their husbands often find slave girls elsewhere—and there are slave-girls and slave-women in every land. This is the law of sensuality.

Romance is the relationship in which man and woman are equal. You may adore your husband no less than he adores you. I am sure that now you show him that you are in love with him in as many ways as he shows you he is in love with you. Don't let that stop. Women who forget it often find that their husbands seek it elsewhere. This is the law of romance.

In loving him you must always be more steadfast than he is. Never doubt him, no matter what the facts may seem to be; love does not doubt. Remember that, no matter what he does, he is yours, and you love him. In this one respect he belongs to you; he is yours to love. Women who do not love their husbands often lose them. This is the law of love.

In sensuality, you are his. In romance, you are equal. In love, he is yours. That is all a bride of three days needs to know, Claire. When Joan and I return from our travels, I will tell you more"

Shortly after his declaration to Joan, Strong had taken Ada to dinner.

"I want to ask you some questions, Ada," he said afterward.

"Ask away."

"I noticed that Hyatt Mansell was paying some attention to you this summer," he continued. "What do you think of him, Ada?"

"I think he is much like you," she answered, "and you know what I think of you, Strong."

"Hyatt and I are much alike, I know. But how are we different?" Strong asked.

Ada thought for a moment.

"Well, there are physical differences, such as age, of course. The two of you are equally attractive, I think, so there is no difference there. Oh, yes—you are a translator and he is a scientist, so your dispositions differ, and you are a woman-hunter and he is an organizer, so your actual occupations are different too. Is that right?"

"Yes, that's right," he responded. "Now, answer one more question. Considering four persons, Hyatt, myself, yourself and Joan, which combinations have matching interests?"

Ada heard what Strong said, saw the truth in it, was undisturbed, for to her Strong and Mansell *were* equally attractive, but she was amused at Strong's approach to the subject.

"Jedediah Strong," she cried in an attempt at heavy drama which was given away by the twinkle in her eye, "are you leaving me for another woman?"

"No, Ada' he replied. "I'm just changing hands."

"What do you mean?" she asked, puzzled.

"Hyatt and I are alike in more ways than you think, Ada," Strong answered. "Our likes and dislikes are almost identical. We are like a right hand and a left hand; what pleases one of us pleases the other. For example, I am attracted to you and to Joan. Without asking him, I know that he is attracted as I am attracted. When for any reason, I must choose between two women, other things being equal, I choose the one whose interests most closely match mine, and I have no doubt that Hyatt does likewise. Did you know he will be here soon?"

"No," said Ada, "I didn't."

"I think Hyatt wants you, Ada," Strong continued. "You share an interest dear to his heart—the Intelligence. The majority of people are interested in the Intelligence only as a means of doing certain things which they consider important; you and Hyatt and a few others are interested in the Intelligence itself as the living brain of the human race. I wish to tell you that I am going away for a year with Joan—and that I think you will find in Hyatt Mansell exactly what you have wanted from me. If you do not, I will be back in a year, and, as I told you once before, I will never let you down. Joan asked me if she might work with me for a long, long time, and I asked her to marry me. Do you think I am neglecting you, Ada?"

"No," she said softly, "I can see that you are not neglecting me, Strong. You're just being gentle and considerate as you always are, and I—well, you know that love is not a dominant part of my nature, but I can say to you honestly that I know now what it is, for I love you."

He took her gently in his arms for a while, and after a deep and tranquil kiss, they parted.

Mansell arrived in New York in time to see Joan and Strong off on their honeymoon. Ada was there too, and the two of them spent the evening together. They had much to talk about. In a week they were daily companions, and Ada was doing her level best to entice the man she now knew she wanted. Nothing happened.

She learned more about the Intelligence every day, and more about her man. The more she knew of him, the more she wanted him—and a strange thing happened. The more she wanted him, the less she felt inclined to entice him. It became too serious for that. She began to see how creative he was, how free from sham, and this produced a change in her.

Within the man she saw his purpose, within the purpose she saw creativeness, and creativeness made her creative. She forgot her personal desires and lost herself in the basic idea of the Intelligence. She thought and thought and thought. One day she said,

"Hyatt, you and Strong have both said that Beauty is the mate of Integrity."

"Yes, Ada," he answered. "So we have."

"Well, I have an idea, Hyatt. Integrity must be measured in time, for time is part of its definition, but beauty is perishable in time and must be judged *now*. It seems to me that it would be a good idea to have personality ratings as well as integrity ratings. They could be an accurate measure of personal attractiveness and charm considered as apart from integrity. Just as now you have places where men and women of high integrity can meet, it would then be possible to have places where men of high integrity and exceptionally beautiful women could meet, as well as places where women of high integrity and exceptionally attractive men could meet. This would make a science out of the matching of Beauty and Integrity, and would rescue those men and women who are most attractive from the spoiled boredom which is their lot at present."

Keeping his voice calm with some little difficulty, Mansell asked,

"How would personality ratings be calculated, Ada?"

"Well," she answered, "personality ratings would not be any indication of wisdom, so there is no reason why they should have any voting power. I think the measure of relative attractiveness should be based upon estimates weighted according to the integrity of the estimators—in other words, the same voting powers as the Intelligence now uses."

Mansell reached forward and took her hands in his.

"Ada," he said, his eyes shining, "you have a brain. Strong and I have talked over the idea of personality ratings, and although we haven't started making any yet, we arrived at the very same conclusions you have just given. Would you like to have a hand in making such ratings and in organizing the gathering-places which they will make possible?"

"When may I start?"

"Now, if you like," he replied. "Come back to the desert with me and we will get to work immediately." Ada's face clouded over.

"Hyatt, I can't," she said sadly. "You forget that I am not yet twenty years of age; my parents simply wouldn't understand."

Hyatt smiled.

"This work is important, Ada; it can't be stopped for that. This calls for strategy."

He was silent for a moment, thinking. Then he looked into her eyes quizzically for a second or two, and smiled suddenly like a small boy planning a raid on the cookie-jar.

"Let's make a conspiracy, Ada. I like you, and I think we understand each other. Your parents are concerned about your security and your safety. We are concerned about working together; we have no designs upon each other. Why don't we get married? It will satisfy your parents, it will enable us to travel and work together, and it need be no more than that. The marriage can be annulled when you are of age, and you will be perfectly free to do as you please."

"I don't intend to live in fire, Hyatt."

"My dear, I think you have good sense; do what you like."

"Hyatt Mansell," Ada said seriously, "do you think I am attractive?"

"You are one of the most magnetic girls I know, Ada. But don't worry about that; I will never bother you."

Ada leaned forward and lowered her voice as if she were telling a great secret.

"There is no way in which you could bother me more, Hyatt," she said slowly.

"What do you mean, Ada? Say it clearly!"

"I mean that I want you, you cautious superman!"

She felt more bare before Mansell than she ever had before Strong.

"I realize that this is to be a marriage of convenience, and that is all right with me because domesticity doesn't interest me anyway. But if we are to have our freedom, must we exclude each other?

You say you like me because my mind shares an interest with yours. That is fine, but I have a body too, and my body wants attention—from you. I have no designs on you, Hyatt—I just want you to take my body as you have taken my mind. Is that wrong?"

The kiss which Ada received in answer to her question was long and thorough, and it seemed as if it took her hours to swim up through many layers of consciousness into the air again. After the bells in her head had stopped ringing, she heard Mansell say,

"We understand each other, Ada. Let us arrange things with your parents and be on our way."

And she was content.

Mr. & Mrs. Jedediah Strong had been married three weeks, and though they slept each night in each other's arms, neither sensuality nor romance had as yet arisen between them. Love blazed between them like a torrent of fire, and lesser forces had to wait their turn.

"Why am I so content with this, Strong?" Joan asked him one day.

"Because the fire of affection which flows between us contains all lesser things and keeps our relationship in perfect balance. If sensuality is within us, it will appear and we shall experience it. Do you really care whether it ever appears or not, Joan?"

"No," she replied thoughtfully, "I don't think I care at all."

"That is one of the curious things about balance," Strong continued. "If sensual desire for you were to arise in me, desire for me would arise in you, that is your balance. But if sensual desire for me were to arise in you, desire for you would arise in me. That is my balance. What do two mirrors see when they face each other? Our relationship is just such a mystery as that.

"We shall see and learn much in our year together, Joan. The life of fire opens many doors, and you will find beyond those doors many things which the world does not believe. You shall see and hear those things, while I will remain blind to them, for I must keep myself in the condition of those who believe nothing. My eyes are the eyes of understanding; your eyes shall be eyes of fire.

In the ideal relationship between man and woman, it is normal for man to excel in integrity and creativeness, while it is normal for woman to excel in sensitivity and awareness; thus the two complete each other."

*****

This book was written in the hope of finding friends for the Intelligence, which is real, though not yet (January 1946) as large as herein described. If you feel yourself to be such a friend, do not conceal the fact; the writer will he pleased to hear from you. At a time when one of the world's most respected governments is planning an experiment (exploding an atomic bomb under water), which is likely to cause more death and destruction than did both world wars, the Intelligence needs friends.

P. B. A.

THE Translator's Press

THE FUSE
An Historical and Philosophical Perspective
MWI Publishing

Beau Kitselman was a mathematical genius who had a lifelong interest in Eastern philosophical teachings and the evolution of human consciousness, a process he referred to as 'integration'.

In 1937, subsequent to his translation of such ancient texts as the Paṭisambhidā Magga from the original Pali, as well as translations of the teachings of the Buddha, Beau began to explore the effects of some of these teachings in a unique way. He took a room at his home, Pyramid Lake Ranch in Nevada (which at this time was called "The Sage") and painted it entirely black. Then, as far as possible, he sound and light proofed it. He then began following the recommendations on meditative practice of the teachers whose writings he had translated as well as doing various yogic postures—all to discover more about this process of integration. These experiments in meditation and sensory deprivation preceded those of John C. Lilly by some 16 years. His experiences during this time led to Beau's first glimpses of what you might call cosmic consciousness and what it might mean to be a fully integrated human being.

Since the early 1930s he had been fascinated by the topic of extrasensory perception, which he called at that time, "hyperconsciounsess" and had written to the famous parapsychologist J.B. Rhine on the topic as early as 1933. He was to later dialogue extensively with Dr Rhine in the early 1960s. His early experiments in extrasensory perception, combined with his study of the writings of Kakusandha, Kapila, Krishna, Lao Tzu, Buddha and Jesus, whom he referred to as the "classical authorities on integration", led to the writing and publication of a book called The Time Teachers in 1939.

In many ways The Fuse is an exposition of some of the concepts and ideas that he had shared in The Time Teachers, but told in semi-fictional form. It was his first and only experiment in using semi-fictional settings and a storytelling process to share deeper fundamental truths about human consciousness and the nature of reality.

Beau had first met the renowned British writer and philosopher, Aldous Huxley, in 1939 whilst he was working in Hollywood. Huxley had written a book, published in 1944, entitled 'Time Must Have a Stop'. Huxley himself thought that this novel was his most successful at "fusing idea with story," and was essentially an experiment in sharing deep philosophical concepts in a fictional form. Its' publication undoubtedly influenced Beau's writing of The Fuse. A number of writers and teachers have discovered that in many ways it is easier to; "share the truth in the form of a lie." Spiritual teacher G. I. Gurdjieff (whose work Beau referenced in his later book E-Therapy) said that:

"By reason of the many characteristics of man's being, particularly of the contemporary being, truth can only come to people in the form of a lie — only in this form are they able to accept it; only in this form are they able to digest and assimilate it. Truth undefiled would be for them, indigestible food."[1]

In essence this book is about 'living in fire' which is a concept that he first explicated in The Time Teachers. In that book he wrote:

"Though these states of concentration may sound abstract, they are a far more common influence in our lives than we are apt to think. Perhaps the oldest name for them is fire; the four shining fires and the four formless fires. It is an instinctive name; it is on our lips frequently when we speak of burning zeal, flaming ardour, 'hot' music, or fiery piano-playing. It is 'fire' that we feel in all our emotional attachments. Excitement, adventure, music, romance, passion, and danger are all means of reaching 'fire'; 'playing with fire' is a phrase which signifies eloquently the strength of the urge. We are all seeking 'fire'; it is just that the common ways are not the best ways."

For most people the only readily available, first-hand experience of fire is through sexual desire and this is where The Fuse begins, with human sexuality. Considering the era in which this book was written, to have such a focus was a brave act, perhaps tempered slightly by the fact that Beau did not publish it under his own name but under the same pseudonym, P.B.A. as he had used when writing The Time Teachers. This pseudonym was in all probability a kind of phonetic acronym derived from the Pali word Paṭisambhidā – PatisamBhidA, which was the title of the basic text that infused The Time Teachers. The word itself is usually translated as 'analytical knowledge,' 'discernment,' or 'discrimination,' though its' literal translation is something like 'thoroughly separate category.' Beau referred to it as 'the flexible method'.

The Fuse is semi-fictional in the sense that Beau changed the names of the characters but the settings were from real-life as well as some, though not all, of the situations. He himself is the main character.

The places in the book are real; as an example; early in the book he says he is taking the three girls to the 'Place of the Ancient Fish' which was 'in the Country of the Water people'. This is a reference to the cui-ui fish and the Lahontan cutthroat trout which were so important to the Northern Paiute Indians of the Pyramid Lake area in Nevada. The word Pai (or Pah) in Paiute is generally understood to mean water. In 1936 Beau had written in an article entitled, "Tibet in America", in which he discussed his discovery of the Pyramid Lake area in Nevada and its potency. The setting of The Fuse is near Pyramid Lake and Sutcliffe, Nevada. His deep love of the area shines through in his description of the Nevada desert. He maintained strong connections with this area until the late 1950s when he moved to Southern California.

Many of the people in the book are real too; the wise elder referred to in the book is Chief Winnemucca and the character called Harvey is undoubtedly Avery Winnemucca.

In the fuse, the character Strong says: "I am an architect; I build persons….I do most of my work for people in creative professions who need to know more about their creative capacities and how to develop them." This is a direct reference to Strong being modelled on Beau himself and the work that he, Beau, and his good friend, the surrealist artist, Salvador de Regil did through their consulting work which they carried out in Hollywood under the name Persons Inc.[2] All the references to the starlet system of the late 1930s and 1940s comes from the work that Beau and Salvador did in Hollywood.

It is fascinating to see the many resonances between the psychological ideas on sexuality and human relationships presented in The Fuse and those of psychiatrist Wilhelm Reich.[3]

In terms of the scientific references in the book, the frequent mention of anti-gravity research comes from Beau's burgeoning friendship with Thomas Townsend Brown, whom he had met whilst they both worked for Lockheed-Vega in the early 1940s. Townsend Brown is famous for his work on the Biefeld-Brown effect with its implications for anti-gravity propulsion systems.[4]

Another key theme in the later part of the book is Beau's concern with the fuse that was lit by man's liberation of atomic energy and his doubts about humanity's ability, at its current level of mental and emotional development, to be able handle it appropriately. A concern shared by many others in the post World War II years and one that led Beau to write directly to Dwight D. Eisenhower in the late 1940s regarding the dangers of deep water atomic testing.

The Fuse was originally published by The Translators Press which was based at 30 East 64th Street in New York City; a somewhat unassuming 17 story skyscraper which contained the Hotel La Salle and which was also the home of one of the oldest metaphysical/spiritual bookstores in the USA. It had originally been called The North Node and then later became the Gateway Bookshop. The author, Alan Watts, wrote in his autobiography that the bookshop was the U.S equivalent of the famous Watkins Bookshop in London and mentions how, in 1939, the owners of the Gateway had helped him to establish himself as a lecturer on spirituality. It seems more than likely that the Gateway bookshop was where Beau and Alan Watts first met. Over the years, the various owners of the bookshop had lived as permanent residents of the Hotel La Salle and it seems that Beau also used the hotel as his base in New York City. This is most likely the same hotel referred to in this novel as being the base of Jedediah Strong in New York.

In 1962, in a brief biography in his last published book Hello Stupid[5], Beau wrote of himself:

"A. L. Kitselman was born in 1914 in the Occident, although he later became an Orientalist. His parents were rich but honest. He idled away his youth reading books, listening to classical music, climbing mountains, loafing, day-dreaming and cooking up half-baked ideas. He was addicted to mathematics, astronomy, philosophy, religion and amateur radio. He squandered his inheritance trying to set up Utopian colonies."

In many ways the book's portrayal of a utopian, counterculture society based in Nevada, foreshadows the now perhaps somewhat infamous counterculture/utopian experiment that has taken place annually there since 1986 called, 'The Burning Man.' This event takes place less than a hundred miles of the area in which The Fuse is set.

We leave it to the reader to research and explore all the many possible resonances and further hidden references in this unique and fascinating text.

Footnotes
1. In Search of the Miraculous by P. D. Ousepnsky
2. See http://www.kitselman.com for more information on Persons Inc.
3. Apart from the similarities with Reich's views on sexuality and human relationships there are also many resonances with some the ideas Reich outlined in such books as Listen Little Man and The Murder of Christ.
4. http://www.thomastownsendbrown.com/'
5. 'Hello Stupid' will be republished by MWI Publishing in e-book format in 2015.

Please visit

http://www.kitselman.com

for more on the life and work of
A. L. Kitselman

and his
"Institute of Integration"

The web site also has audio lectures
by Kitselman
on the
"Classical Authorities on Integration"

Discover more writings by
A. L. Kitselman
overleaf

Tao Teh King

Since the 1970s, the influence of oriental philosophy, in particular the Buddhist tradition, in the field of psychotherapy has been quite profound. Taoism has not had the same impact on modern psychotherapeutic models. Yet, as early as 1936, Alva LaSalle Kitselman who was, at that time, studying oriental languages at Stanford University, with a particular emphasis on Sanskrit, created his own version of the classic text of the Taoist tradition - the book of Lao Tzu entitled the *Tao Teh King*. His version of this classic was, as he said, a restatement rather than being a new translation from the ancient Chinese. After its publication, and through a chance encounter with one of the librarians at Stanford, he began to realise that Taoism and Taoist philosophy could be used as a form of therapy, specifically in the form he called 'non-directiveness' or 'non-directive therapy.'

In the 1950s Kitselman published an audio lecture on his early experiences using the Tao Teh King entitled 'An Ancient Therapy'. In the lecture he compared and contrasted his application of Taoist philosophy in psychotherapy with the 'client centred therapy' approach of Carl R. Rogers. This new publication of Kitselman's version of the Tao Teh King and the story of his discovery will hopefully ignite a real interest in combining the wisdom of this classic Taoist text with modern psychotherapeutic methodologies.text with modern psychotherapeutic methodologies.

Hardback with over 40 black and white photographs.
ISBN: 978-0-9565803-9-9

The Time Teachers

Following a long series of successful experiments in 1933, aimed at predicting the results of a simple coin toss, A. L. Kitselman realized that human consciousness must be able to operate outside of the constraints of time and space.

Concurrent with these experiments and in the years that followed his study of the ancient teachers of philosophy and religion, such as Kakusandha, Krishna, Buddha, Lao Tzu and Jesus, convinced him that all these teachers had a deep appreciation of the capacity of human consciousness to operate outside of time and space.

In this book Kitselman outlines a unique approach to training the human mind to enhance internal integration and achieve self mastery. He draws strongly on the Theravada Buddhist tradition as outlined in the Paṭisambhidāmagga or Path of Discernment.

Paperback
ISBN-13: 978-1501038938

E-Therapy

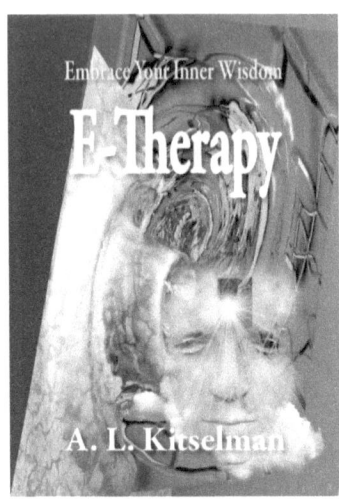

Would you like to ..

Improve your conduct? Is there a habit you'd like to get rid of?

Experience extreme physical pleasure? Intense, ever-fresh happiness? Deep impartial calmness?

Lose the feeling of insecurity? Make an end of doubt and perplexity? Lose all sense of fear, hatred, and grief?

Become a prodigy in science, government, business, art or education? A genius in originality, mental grasp, or in understanding others? Would you like to develop supernormal powers?

Become fully integrated? To be directly aware of things (without needing to sense them or think about them)? To realize a state of being in which there is no obstruction?

These pages tell how.
with a new introduction by Suzette Kitselman

Paperback (also on kindle)
ISBN: 978-0-9565803-7-5

E-Therapy Lectures

What Integration is About
The Four Unthinkables
The Easiest Way

The Institute of Integration, founded by A. L. Kitselman in the early 1950s, produced a large library of audio tapes on personal psychological integration. Kitselman felt that three of those lectures, concerning the process of integration through 'E-Therapy,' were of such significant and special interest as to warrant printing them in booklet form in 1960.

This volume faithfully reproduces those lectures—What Integration is About, The Four Unthinkables and The Easiest Way, as well as including a new introduction to her father's work by his daughter Khema Rani Kitselman.

Paperback (kindle version available)
ISBN: 978-0-9565803-8-2